Compton-Burnett, Ivy
    The last and the first.

DATE DUE			
Jan. 5	Sept. 14		
Jan. 28	Sept. 22		
Feb. 19	Oct. 2		
Mar. 4	NOV 13 1972		
Mar. 16	APR 17 78		
Apr. 14	DEC 11		
MAY 5 1972			
Apr. 21			
June 1			
June 8			
June 20			
Aug. 3			

THE LAST
AND
THE FIRST

THE LAST
AND
THE FIRST

I. COMPTON–BURNETT

ALFRED A. KNOPF
NEW YORK
1971

British Publisher's Note

After Dame Ivy Compton-Burnett died, in August, 1969, it was found that she had appointed no literary executor. It has therefore fallen to her British publisher to prepare her final manuscript for press. For assistance in this work I am much indebted to Miss Cicely Greig (who has typed Dame Ivy's manuscripts for very many years), Miss Elizabeth Sprigge, and Mr. Charles Burkhart, all of whom have made suggestions which have been most valuable in deciding on the text printed here.

Only essential editing has been done, and this, in the main, to correct obvious slips in the text (such as "step-daughter" to replace an erroneous "step-mother," etc.). In addition, one short but necessary bridge passage was constructed.

Of the manuscript, Elizabeth Sprigge writes: "Ivy began The Last and the First *during the summer of 1964. In April, 1965 she wrote to Miss Greig, 'My novel is still in an early stage, and I myself disabled by a mild heart trouble, and have to be slow.'*

"Nineteen sixty-five was a difficult year for Ivy even before her first accident. She had several changes of housekeeper; in June 'a cough and domestic changes' were worrying her and Julian Mitchell's dramatisation of her novel A Heritage and Its History, *of which she wholly approved, involved a great deal of correspondence.*

"In June, 1969 she spoke of her 'little book' to Miss Greig again. She was depressed about it and Miss Greig begged to be allowed to type the script as far as it went, feeling that it would help Ivy to be able to read a clear copy of what she had

written. Ivy, however, refused to have any of it typed until it was finished and warned Miss Greig that it would be 'a terrible manuscript, so much crossed out.'

"Most of the script in the earlier notebooks is in the small firm handwriting that Ivy reserved for her books, so although there are indeed many crossings out, it is fairly easy to decipher. Much of the final notebook is a scribble and contains loose pages in the large frail tired handwriting of her last days. Often the pages appear out of sequence, and there seem to be some missing. There are also a few passages and odd words here and there which do not fit into the text and would presumably have been altered or omitted had Ivy been able to revise the script. These have been fitted where possible and otherwise omitted. The last pages of the manuscript are, however, in the earlier small neat writing, indicating that they were composed earlier. Apart from the few sentences mentioned, the whole script has been meticulously transcribed with faithful adherence to the original."

London, 1970   LIVIA GOLLANCZ

THE LAST
AND
THE FIRST

ONE

"What an unbecoming light this is!" said Eliza Heriot, looking from the globe above the table to the faces round it.

"Are we expected to agree?" said her son, as the light fell on her own face. "Or is it a moment for silence?"

"The effect is worse with every day. I hardly dare look at any of you."

"You have found the courage," said her daughter, "and it is fair that you should show it. You appointed the breakfast hour yourself."

Lady Heriot did not suggest that anyone else should appoint it.

"Well, good morning to you all," she said, her plural phrase suggesting she did not greet rare creatures. "So you are all in time to-day."

"As we are on most days," said her son. "You imply a thing that is not."

"Good-morning, Mater," said the younger of her step-daughters, her quiet tone challenging any cause for criticism. "Yes, we are all in time, and happy in the fire-light until the daylight intervenes."

"The fire must have been lighted early to be as forward as this," said Eliza, with her eyes on it. "I must go into the matter later."

"The fire in this grate is never slow," said her elder step-daughter. "It was cold and black when I saw it half-an-hour ago."

"I will go into the matter later," said Eliza, as though untouched by the words.

"It takes time for a fire to grow. If it fails in that purpose it is lost in another way. It is another kind of waste."

"I will go into the matter later," said her step-mother. "Hermia, do you eat no fat at all?"

"None, as you know. I am not a stranger to you."

"Well, you almost are," said Eliza with a sigh. "I hardly understand this intensity of feeling over food. It is not such a great matter."

"I might say the same to you. Though we are talking of fat not food."

"Well-behaved people betray no feeling about such things."

"Likes and dislikes go a little deeper than that, Mater," said Madeline.

"Nothing goes deeper than manners," said Eliza, in an instructive tone. "They are involved with the whole of life. It is they that give rise to it, and come to depend on it. We should all remember it."

"It might be well to forget it," said her son, "if it in any way suggests the whole of life. Our own share of that is enough, and we know you are equal to the rest."

Eliza almost laughed at the compliment in the words, and turned her eyes in maternal feeling on her own children, her expression revealing that it was strong and deep. She was a fair, almost handsome woman of fifty-five, with solid aquiline features and a short, upright frame, and active hands that seemed their natural complement.

Her daughter and second child was like and unlike her, with another strain showing in her lighter form and face, and something both weaker and stronger in the impression she made.

The only son, Angus, was as short for a man as his

4

mother for a woman, broad and heavy and almost plain, with a likeness to his father that gave him his family place. They both had more expressive eyes than Eliza, grey in Roberta and hazel in Angus; and Roberta had also what were known as the Heriot hands, while Angus's recalled Sir Robert's. Though now between the ages of twenty and twenty-four, they were conscious of Eliza and under constraint in her presence.

Hermia, her elder step-daughter, bore the strongest likeness to the father, which was noted by strangers and ignored by Eliza, who passed over family resemblances, was indeed hardly alive to them. Hermia was a tall, dark, restless woman of thirty-four, with a look of being personally unusual, inherited from her father and recognised by herself. She looked her full age and saw nothing against it, indeed had this attitude to most of what she was and did, but failed to share it with Eliza who simply saw no ground for it.

Madeline, four years younger, was taller and fairer and more ordinary, with pale eyes, a compressed nose and mouth, long, rather lifeless hands and limbs and her own self-esteem, which Eliza was inclined to accept, indeed almost saw as justified.

The power in the family was vested in Eliza, as her husband left it wholly in her hands, and had moreover willed the property to her, in trust at her death, but subject to her control during her life. She wielded the power as she thought and meant, wisely and well, but had not escaped its influence. Autocratic by nature, she had become impossibly so, and had come to find criticism a duty, and even an outlet for energy that had no other.

Hermia resented her power and her use of it, and failed to grasp her father's feeling for her; and Madeline cultivated an affection for her, feeling it in some way a tribute to herself. That their father would hardly have made the will if he had fully known her was believed by Hermia and suspected by her children, though it had not occurred to herself.

Sir Robert Heriot entered the room, an impressive old man, looking less than his eighty-two years, and otherwise much as the father of Angus and Hermia would be expected to look. He took the seat at his wife's side, renouncing the end of the table, and leaving other places empty, as she would assign them to no one else. Roberta had the seat on his other hand, by virtue of being his chosen child. The position was accorded her by her mother, and could not be questioned, as the date was that of her birth.

"Hermia," said Eliza, "I gave you money to pay the tradespeople, on your errand to the village yesterday."

"They were paid," said Hermia.

"I have a sense of grievance," said Eliza, in a light tone. "Something must be owing to me."

"Often an untrue belief, Mater," said Hermia. "This time it is not. I left your change in the library."

Eliza signed to her son, who left the room. There was a pause.

"And I took it to pay a parish subscription," said Madeline. "Angus is perplexed and taking time to find it."

Her brother returned and laid some coins at his mother's hand.

"Why, where did you get it, my boy?"

"Oh— Hermia said the library."

"It was not there. It had been taken and used."

"Oh well, I thought you wanted it."

"Not those particular coins. Just some change for my purse. Why did you not say it was not there?"

"Oh, I thought perhaps it ought to be."

6

"What an empty episode!" said Eliza. "It seems to have no meaning."

"It has none," said Sir Robert. "So we will not give it one. We will not pretend that something has happened when nothing has. Another time deal openly, my son."

"As things are, Angus is paying the subscription," said Madeline.

"I will pay it as a penalty. I took too much on myself. It is all a storm in a teacup."

"If it stays there," said Roberta. "I never think teacups can be equal to the tempests they contain."

Eliza used another tone. "Did you have a fire in your room last night, Hermia? I saw the ashes in the grate as I passed the door."

"Then you know I had one. And you must have opened the door. I shut it when I came down."

"I open any door in my house when and where I please. That is not what I said. I asked if you had a fire in your room, and I am waiting for an answer."

"There is no need of one. You have seen that I did. It was too cold to be without one."

"Did you ask me if you could have a fire? You know my rule."

"The words would have had no meaning."

"You gave an order to servants of mine in my house, and said no word on the matter. What can be said to that?"

There was a pause, and Sir Robert looked down with a disturbed expression. He was normally on the side of his wife, hardly believing that she could be wrong, and caring especially for her children; but he kept the feelings of a father and the memory of the days when Hermia stood high in his life.

"This house is my home," said his daughter. "I remain

7

in it as I have no other. I am entitled to human comfort under its roof."

"Oh, come, you will have to meet each other," said her father. "Hermia will ask you another time, and you will arrange what she needs. That settles it for both of you."

"If I feel disposed to arrange it. It is for me to decide. Whose house is it? Hers or mine?"

"Yours in the main. And a little everyone else's as well. If you will allow it to be. And we know you will. We know you better than you know yourself. We have learned where to put our trust."

"I feel that is true," said Eliza. "Or it is not without its truth. It is what gives me my place, and makes it possible for me. I don't mean that I would change it. I chose it, and it is mine. And you would see it simply as the best in the house. And that is what it is; that is why it can be no one else's. But the yoke is not always easy, or the burden light."

"Why is it not the best?" said Angus. "It is the choice many people would make."

"Not many people, my boy, if they knew it and knew themselves. But they don't know either. The surface is what they see. Is my own son among them?"

"The surface might easily be seen," said Roberta. "It is hardly a thing to pass over."

"I admit that I see it," said Angus. "I should delight to have a place of power, and fall into the pitfalls that beset it."

"As I do, my son?" said Eliza, half sadly. "As I do, I suppose? Well, I must try to do better. And you will all try to do better too. We will all try together. It is not only your mother who has pitfalls in her path."

"No one can do much in daily life," said Madeline. "We simply do our best in the sphere that happens to be ours."

"Not a very great best is asked of you," said Eliza, with a faint smile. "I sometimes wonder if I am right in letting you all go on so easily, taking everything and giving nothing, indeed having nothing asked of you. But I don't see how I can help it, being as I am. I am not a person to expect much. Perhaps I have learned not to be. If a mistake is being made, it is mine."

"We take the necessities of life," said Hermia. "And ask nothing beyond them. It is Father who gives us everything we have. We take nothing from anyone else."

"How material things fill your horizon!" said Eliza, in a musing tone, resting her eyes on her step-daughter. "I should not have thought they would loom so large. They never have with me. But I may not be like other people. I begin to see I am not. You forget the effort and thought that support the even tenor of your life. But what your father has and can give you would be of little good without them."

"We could manage for ourselves if things were in our hands. There would be no trouble."

"Well, they are not in your hands," said Eliza, with a little laugh. "It is a contingency that need not be considered, as it will not arise. Who and what do you imagine you are?"

"I know what I am. A woman of thirty-four, with no scope and no chance of having any. It is not likely I should forget. Would it often be out of my mind?"

"What are your ideas for your life?" said Sir Robert, whose eyes were on her. "It seems you must have them, if you have thought and felt as you say. Put it in words that we understand. We are in the dark."

"I will lighten your darkness. I could hardly not have my ideas. There has been time to form them. They have come to be comprised in a wish for a definite thing. The

9

large school in the town is not doing well, and the principal would like a partner. It would mean an outlay, but not, I believe, a prohibitive one. If that could be managed for me, I should be happier and more useful. I feel I have no place here."

"What kind of place do you want?" said Eliza. "You share the family home and life. Why have you a right to more? And the position would not be the same. You will be seen in another way. You would have to be prepared for it."

"I don't know how I am seen now. Or rather I do know; it is as I see myself. And I am ready for it to end." Hermia kept her eyes turned from Eliza as she voiced unutterable words. "The household will be happier without me. I can only be a discordant element. I am a reminder to Mater of the life Father had before he knew her. And a reminder to him of it too. And it is often in my own mind. How often no one knows."

"Of course no one does," said Eliza. "No one knows what is in anyone else's mind. You don't know what is in mine; you do not indeed. And why should people think about your mind? Do you give a thought to theirs? Perhaps they are hardly as much concerned with you as you are with yourself."

"We know your views," said Hermia's father. "But think before you give up your home and your place in it. They are things that do not come again."

"I know that, Father. I am ready to give them up. I feel I have hardly had them."

"You have had the place that was yours. Mater has given it to you, given it for all these years. You must recognise it, Hermia. What have you given in return? No one would choose to have step-children."

"I have given nothing. I have had nothing to give. And who would choose to have a step-mother? There was no choice for either of us there. We have done what we were forced to do. Mater may be grateful to me for going. That is where the gratitude will lie.

"I don't know why my name is brought into this," said Eliza, in a cold tone. "I have nothing to do with it. The change is being made without reference to me. Hermia has had her full rights here. She would have had no more with her own mother. I don't know why she is a martyr."

"She is not," said Sir Robert. "She is an able young woman, who needs an outlet for her gifts. Her energy has been accumulating and has broken forth. That is all it is."

"Gifts?" said Eliza, drawing in her brows. "Are they to be depended on? Does she know what they are?"

"She may. And others will know, when she begins to use them. We shall hear of her success, if it comes. And she will have her freedom, if that is what it is. Some people would give it another name."

"They would and will. That is a thing she will have to face. I don't know how she will like it. From what I know of her, not much."

"I shall not know anything about it," said Hermia. "No one will say the thing to me. Or I shall not be at home to hear them. And the people I am with will not say them. I shall be quite safe."

"I don't know why I am regarded like this," broke out Eliza. "As someone who has failed in some way, when what I have done is to think and manage more than other people. I wish I had not done it. I would not do it again. I will not go on doing it. I will follow Hermia's example and think of myself. And the result for other people need not matter to me. It does not matter to her."

She sank into tears, and her husband rose and put his arm about her, signing to his children to leave them.

TWO

THEY WITHDREW TO a refuge at the back of the hall, a small room furnished with discards from other rooms with a view to their occupation of it.

"Well, Mater is weeping on Father's shoulder," said Hermia. "Over a change that is as welcome to her as it is to me. I might as well cry over it myself."

"If she is we can only regret it," said Madeline. "It is not a good opening to a new regime."

"Mater sees and hears herself," said Hermia. "That ends my pity for her, and transfers it to Father. He sees and hears her too."

"I feel pity for all of us," said Angus. "How could we know what was in store? If Hermia escapes without further stress she has done better than I could have believed. I realise her courage and my want of it."

"Suppose we all had it!" said Roberta. "It may be a good thing it is rare."

"If courage is the word," said Madeline.

"I can hardly believe in what I did," said Hermia. "I could not do it again."

"I am glad of that," said Angus.

"You need not fear. I feel that virtue has gone out of me. All that was in me. There is nothing left."

"If that is the word again," said Madeline. "It is perhaps not the only one."

"I don't mind about the word. You will have to show the quality. You are to inherit my place and be a success in it. You can hardly be more of a failure."

"I have my own place," said Madeline quietly. "And it may be better for other people for me to keep it."

"It is," said Angus. "We value its protection."

"The blank I leave has always been there," said Hermia. "My thoughts have been on my own problems. On myself, if you like it better. I am not ashamed of it."

"You evidently are," said Roberta. "I suppose it shows that no one is all bad."

"Why is it wrong to think of oneself? What is more natural and more necessary?"

"We do what is natural to us," said Madeline. "Obedience to our natures. It is a part of life."

"A very small part," said Roberta.

"Nearly the whole of life."

"A very good thing it is," said Angus. "It is what prevents its being quite the whole of other people's lives."

"It is the whole of mine," said Hermia. "Nothing could be a preventive. It has not been even a part of it. I am to have it at last. I can hardly believe it."

"I can believe it," said Roberta. "I think we have evidence of it."

"It is a great deal to have," said Angus. "And the evidence is on a scale with it."

"Father will miss Hermia," said Madeline, somehow suggesting Eliza's possible doubt of it.

"And will not be allowed to show it," said her sister. "And will be well advised not to."

"We shall all be more exposed," said Angus. "I can no longer rejoice as a young man in my youth."

"Suppose I had rejoiced in mine," said Hermia. "What a difference there would be! I might want to cling to it."

"I never think about my youth or my age," said Madeline. "I feel such things are out of our hands."

"Your impression is a right one," said Roberta. "But that is what is wrong with them. We can do nothing."

"Mater and I should never meet again," said Hermia. "I wish our family ran on normal lines."

"You have much to face," said Angus. "But so has she. A daughter leaving the family home to seek employment! It is not a thing she would be proud of."

"There is no cause for pride. It has never been a home to me."

"Then what has it been?" said her father at the door. "How have you used it?"

"As a place where she is cooked for and cared for and provided with anything she pleases," said Eliza. "What would that be but a home? The school will do it for her in return for what she does herself, the last thing that has happened here. And the effort will be real if the scheme is not to founder and fail. And it must not fail, Hermia. The money can ill be spared. And things will not be what you are used to. The change will be great."

"She is prepared for it," said Sir Robert. "She is willing for effort, and it is true that none has been asked of her here. When she returns she will be welcomed as a daughter, if not the first and foremost one; that place she is passing on. But I think with her eyes open. She knows her mind."

"The work I am to do will not be for myself," said Hermia. "There need be no fear that I shall lead a self-indulgent life."

"I do not fear it," said Eliza. "My fear takes another line. Will it be self-indulgent enough? Will the difference be too much? You will have to adapt yourself to other people, the thing you have never done. The parents of the pupils will have a right to criticise. You will be in a sense employed. From what I have seen you will not suffer it gladly."

14

"I shall not suffer it at all. I shall take a high hand. It makes people think more of you."

"You have a good deal to learn," said Sir Robert, smiling. "It may do you no harm to learn it. Though you might have gone through your life without doing so. You are taking the hard way. You don't seem well suited to the easy one. It needs its own qualities."

"I am glad to hear that," said Angus. "As I am so very well suited to it."

"There is enough for you to do," said his father. "And it will be more with time."

"That is what I am afraid of. It may."

"My Angus!" said Eliza. "The demands on him will grow, and he will grow with them. And he will always be his mother's son."

"But can I take a place in the world by being that? There would have to be a good many."

"You should follow my example," said Hermia, "and go out into the world."

"It must be at less expense," said Eliza. "And is it an example that leads to a place in the world? It seems to be a costly way of dispensing with one. Have you any idea what your duties are to be? What a change it will be for you! Do you know how a school is run?"

"Well, my thoughts have been on it of late. And I see what mistakes are being made, and how they could be rectified."

"Ah, that is how we all begin," said her father. "We see what is wrong on the surface and forget all that lies underneath, indeed may be unconscious of it. Well, the first steps have to be taken. The others may follow."

"I feel I have ability that has not been used. I have seen the working of this house, and know how I should manage it if it were mine."

15

"Well, we are glad it is not yours. We are grateful for the way it is managed. And so should you be, as it has been done partly for you."

"You would have done better in my place?" said Eliza. "I might say the same to you. I can state an honest opinion. You make no secret of yours."

"My powers have had to lie fallow. I have given no impression of myself."

"The first may be true," said Sir Robert. "And the second part of the truth. But powers that have not been used have not been tried."

"And not only powers are in question," said Eliza. "There are other things to be taken into account. Powers are not the whole of anyone. They may be a small part. And we all give an impression of ourselves, whether we think it or not."

"And our powers are needed in our daily life," said Madeline. "There is really a constant use for them."

"Have you found it so with Hermia's?" said Eliza.

"It is fair to say that I have, Mater. I have gained a support from them, and shall miss it when she goes. But they may not have been put to their full use."

"Surely that was full enough," said Angus.

"It would have served," said his father.

"It had to, Father," said Hermia. "It will now be fuller and more definite. I have to justify your faith in me."

"His faith in you?" said Eliza, just drawing in her brows. "I thought he seemed to have misgivings."

"I had them and still have them," said Sir Robert. "As I have said, unused powers are not proved. She is showing courage."

"A quality she has had no reason to show so far. It has indeed not been proved."

"I don't know," said Sir Robert, with a smile. "Perhaps it has been to-day."

"Oh, I am not an autocrat. There was nothing to be afraid of."

"What did you say, Mater?" said Angus. "You should think before you speak."

"You all call me Mater now," said Eliza with a frown. "The name was chosen for Hermia and Madeline, because they remembered their own mother. There is no point in it for anyone else."

"But it is better not to have two names," said Madeline. "And Mater has the maternal implication, and yet seems to avoid the deeper one. No doubt that was how Father thought of it."

"It may have been," said Sir Robert. "Anyhow it is established by usage."

"Well, Mater or not, I am no tyrant," said Eliza. "People are not afraid of me. Sometimes, I think, too little."

"That is not likely," said Hermia. "Fear goes a long way. I may or may not have courage, but I have not been quite free from it. I have been afraid of provoking your outbreaks. Perhaps more than of the outbreaks themselves. You may have made me afraid of myself."

"Mater will soon be afraid of Hermia," murmured Roberta.

"The outbreaks, as you call them, have their reason," said Eliza. "Things that are wrong must be rectified."

"Whatever I call them, they add to the wrong."

"I did not know you were so much on the side of righteousness! I have not recognised the signs of it."

"Most of us are on its side in a way."

"Do you mean that I am not?"

"I daresay you believe you are. That is also true of most of us."

17

"You take this occasion to say things you would not say on any other," said Madeline. "You have caused it yourself. You should take no advantage of it."

"They were innocent things to say. I might always have said them."

"They were the most guilty things," murmured Angus to Roberta. "And if she might have said them, we know she would have."

"We are all afraid of Mater. Have we to be afraid of Hermia too? It is a pity they are not afraid of each other. I can't think why they are not."

"How soon is Hermia going?" said Madeline. "There will have to be adjustments in the house. I suppose she will take her books with her?"

"Yes, I shall," said her sister. "They are all that I need to take."

"They are all she has a right to take," said Eliza, with a faint smile. "Roberta is to have her room. I have always imagined her in it. And if I had been like other women, she would always have had it. There need be no discussion or question. The matter is settled."

"Would not Madeline like to have the room?" said Hermia.

"You heard what I said. The room is to be Roberta's. She will have some advantage at last. I will hear nothing against it."

"There is nothing against it, Mater," said Madeline, gently. "I am quite content with my room. It has some-how become a part of me. That is a thing a room can do. I will help her to move into the other."

"You have the stronger claim," said Angus.

"No one has any claim," said Eliza. "The room is mine, like everything else in the house. And I am giving it to Roberta. When Hermia comes home she can have

18

one of the spare rooms. She can move into the smaller one tomorrow. That is her place in the house now. It is the one she has chosen herself. She wishes to be a guest and she can be one."

"My place is to know me no more," said Hermia. "And the small spare room does not know me either. So I shall be a stranger here. And there need be no talk of the past, as that would mean I was something else. I leave the house, the past forgetting, by the past forgot."

"Come, what shallow, showy talk!" said Sir Robert. "You sound as if you were not human, and as if no one else was human either. We don't forget thirty-four years. You know you have not forgotten them."

"Not the first ten of them, Father. They are often in my mind. They are what I take with me."

"The first ten years of life are largely forgotten by everyone," said Eliza.

"Not by me. The change that came then cut them off and defined the memory."

"Such a memory is chiefly made up of what is heard later."

"Not in my case. It could not be. I have heard nothing of those years since they ended. They have hardly been mentioned."

"Well, should they have been? No one was thinking of them."

"You can't really believe that."

"I know it. No one could know it better. Who should know as well as I?"

"The two who were thinking of them, and think of them still. And will always think of them."

"I know what your father is thinking. His mind is an open book to me. And you said yourself that those years were never mentioned. If he was thinking of them, they would have been."

"They would not, as you know. You know they could not be. You know they can't be now. The silence deepens the thought."

"I am giving up," said Eliza. "It is all too much. First, I have to be a step-mother, and put other children before my own. And then I am a tyrant, because I order the house for the good of us all. And now I can be dealt with as if years of thought and care had not been lived. I have indeed struck a rough road. Well, it is mine, and I must follow it."

"Oh, come, you are overwrought," said Sir Robert. "Of course you must follow it. Hermia is not to set a fashion. We could not get along it without you. All roads have their stony places. We don't look for life to be smooth."

"Why not?" said Roberta. "We are told that it is sweet. It is not fair that it should be so different."

"That means life as opposed to death," said Madeline.

"Well, anything might be sweet as opposed to that," said Angus.

"No, I don't agree. I can think of many things that would not. Death is anyhow natural and innocent."

"And that is not much to be. The most congenial things may be neither."

"And seldom both," said Hermia. "I hardly think ever."

"When will you be going to the school?" said Madeline, as if willing to change the talk. "It is best to know in good time."

"As soon as I can. I should be there before the term. There will be things to learn before I can take my part in it."

"There will be one thing," said Eliza. "How to consider a number of people besides yourself. It would be less of a change for me."

"Suppose you succeed in persuading me to stay! How will you feel then?"

20

"It is your life we are talking of, not mine."

"We are talking of them both. They have been involved with each other. And it is better that they should not be. That is surely clear."

"You are not being driven from your home. I will neither admit it nor have it said. And people are so prone to say that kind of thing."

"Well, they would find it congenial. It is a normal human tendency. And I don't care what they say."

"When I have said I do care, that is not the right feeling. Well, may your indifference serve you in your new world. May you maintain it in the face of its trials. You have not shown it in much lesser ones here."

"She may find it a help," said Sir Robert. "She must know how to use it, and how not to misuse it. She must do both."

"I have always done both, Father."

"You are wrong. You have only done one," said Eliza. "You are only doing one now."

"Well, it is settled," said Sir Robert. "We will leave the subject."

"We will not," said Angus. "We will continue it and return to it, and prove our appreciation of it. Subjects are rare things."

"That may be as well," said Roberta. "We could become exhausted before they were themselves. It is a thing a subject never seems to be."

"Well, Hermia is to leave us," said Sir Robert. "But she is not going far. She will come home, and we may go to her. I don't know the customs of a school."

"They will not want us there," said Eliza. "We should serve no purpose for them. That is how they would see it. Hermia will come and go here as she wishes. That need not be said."

"I am glad to feel it," said Hermia. "It will give me a background and a better place. I am not blind to it."

"If you are not I wonder you want the change."

"Well, she does want it," said Sir Robert. "She must remember it will not always be a change. Nothing can be blamed for that, though many things are."

Eliza turned to the door, as though choosing to leave the matter, and signed to her husband to come with her. The elder daughters followed, and her own two children were alone.

"What do you think of the family scenes, Roberta? Do you feel degraded by them?"

"No, I feel I am above them. Degradation would become a normal state."

"If only Mater could accept her life! She is really her own worst enemy. And I thought that was just a saying."

"It is. Like everyone else she is her own best friend. But that is not to say there might not be a better."

"Does Father understand the inner truth of things?"

"No, she is too wise, and so is he."

"Would you like to make your escape?"

"What would be gained? It would be freedom and nothing else. Hermia's escape is accepted and given support. And Madeline is proud of not wishing to make an escape. And I see it is a cause for pride. I could not emulate either."

"What do you feel about Hermia's desertion?"

"I am very much affected by it. I see that you are too. And we shall not have our mother's sympathy."

"Father will not have it either. I wonder how much he wants it. Does he often return to the past?"

"It seems to me that he must. If I had a past I would return to it."

"We should be founding one for ourselves. Here is

Mater to give her help. How she will improve and embitter it!"

"So you are still here," said Eliza. "What are you discussing with such gravity?"

"What you know we are," said Angus. "What you know we must be. What you would not believe we were not."

"Well, what do you think of Hermia's scheme?"

"What you do, and what Father does, and what she does herself. We think it all. We are full of thought."

"What do you really think? That tells me nothing."

"Oh, I thought it told you everything."

"Do you feel that her going is my fault? I know it will be said to be."

"It is the fault of us all. We have failed to attach her to us. The surprising thing must be said."

"It is all that will be said, I see. Well, I suppose it is true. But we are all involved. It is not only I who have failed. What are we to say to people about it all?"

"Nothing," said Roberta. "Silence can say more than words. It will say that we are greatly upset and embarrassed by it. And that is much more than words. We know they would not say it."

"Suppose they did!" said Angus. "But we will not suppose it."

"We will not. Imagining something is said to lead to acting on it. Here are Hermia and Madeline and someone with them. It is Mrs. Duff with some matter of daily life."

"We are sorry to disturb you, Mater," said Madeline, accepting the check imposed by their presence. "There is something that needs your attention."

"A good many things do that. I suppose I must hear of this one."

"Yes, a moment, if you please, my lady," said another

voice, as there appeared a middle-aged woman in undisguisedly working garb, with an inharmonious face and a responsible aspect. "If there was not a word to be said I would not say it."

"Why, what is it, Mrs. Duff?" said Eliza, her manner smoother to her housekeeper than it often was to her family. "I hope there is nothing wrong."

"If I have said it once, my lady, I have said it again. 'Something will occur,' I have said. Those have been my words."

"But what has occurred?" said Eliza.

"I am not one to stand by as if nothing was of any account. Self may be in our minds, but need not be uppermost."

"Well, what is in your mind now as well as self?" said Angus. "It is to your credit that there is room for it."

"The back staircase, sir, the broken step. It has cried out for repair. 'We have only to wait,' I said. 'Something must ensue.' And it proved an apt comment."

"You did not wait in vain," said Roberta. "Something has ensued. I hope not a great thing. I suppose there is a human victim."

"Well, it is Agnes, the under-housemaid, miss," said Mrs. Duff, as if the position did amount to this. "And we must accept it as an incident."

"But what is it? Is the girl much hurt?"

"Well, it is hard to say, miss. They make the most of it. Her account is only her own."

"Should we send for the doctor?" said Angus.

"The message has been despatched, sir. I took it on myself. And after your usual exchange a word can ensue on Agnes. It may be all that is called for."

"It is a tiresome thing to happen," said Eliza.

"Well, my lady, the term may suffice."

"I will arrange for the staircase to be mended."

"It takes an incident, my lady, to lead to the point of preventing them. But better late than never."

"I will come and see Agnes."

"Well, attention is focused on her, my lady. And enough is as good as a feast. There will be the natural effect."

"She had better rest for a few days."

"There are light duties, my lady. And things to be done for Miss Hermia before she goes. If she will have the same needs in her new life as she has had in this one."

"We don't know much about the new life. We have only just heard of it."

"Yes, my lady, it is outside your range," said Mrs. Duff in a tone of sympathy as she withdrew. "There is a difference in spheres that you would be alive to."

"Does Mrs. Duff listen at doors?" said Angus. "Or has she powers of her own?"

"Most of them listen," said Eliza. "They see no harm in it."

"What harm does it do them? I should see the good in it."

"The village carpenter can do the repair. The appearance does not matter for the back staircase."

"Its users are entitled to safety, and nothing further."

"They will not mind. They come from simple homes. Mrs. Duff has done better with her opportunities than you are doing with yours, Hermia."

"I may use them, now they have come. I have her example before me."

"I wonder if you could say what they will be. Well, it is no good to talk about it."

"None. If it was any good a fair amount would be done by now."

Eliza walked out of the room as if she had not heard, and Madeline spoke in a grave tone.

"Hermia, must you go to such lengths with Mater? I don't mean you should not say what you feel, but there is reason in everything."

"Then what do you mean? I say just what I feel."

"There is no need to show yourself in this light. It will leave such a sorry memory."

"It will leave a right one. I have always said it in my heart. And as I am going I dare to voice it. And I should not have escaped without doing so. I see what my bonds have been. And I see they are barely broken."

"We saw them being assailed and wrenched apart," said Angus. "And we see no one else will ever break them."

"There must be bonds in every life," said Madeline. "There are things in all of us that prove we need them."

"There are," said Sir Robert's voice. "And you must cease to break them, Hermia. You are having your wish granted, in the face of Mater's doubt and mine, and should be grateful to me, and more to her. I should not have granted it, if she had pressed her view. She is showing forbearance and tolerance. What are you showing?"

"Neither at the time. But I have had to show them. And I should have to show them again. What I am showing is a resolve to live my own life according to myself. Whose life is it but mine? I am forced to show it and to go on showing it. I should be grateful to pursue my way in peace. There seems no end to it."

"Well, well, there is an end. You have faced us and conquered us, and take the spoils of the victor. We may live to see you are wise. We hope we shall, my dear. That we did not want the change does not mean we don't want your success in it. We want it as much as you do. You take that knowledge with you."

He left them, as if bringing the matter to a fitting end, and Angus spoke at once.

"I wished I dared to praise myself. It seems a family gift. Father and Mater and Hermia all have it. And I think Madeline has it in a way of her own."

"Then I should not ever use it. I am quite aware I am not all that I should be."

"I am so much more than I should be that I am ashamed of it. I have the gift after all, and can use it."

"We are all ashamed of it," said Roberta. "There is no credit in not being free. If the compulsions of our life were lifted, I wonder what would break forth. It might not be a case for the family gift."

"It might not," said Madeline. "Father is right. A certain amount of restraint is a safeguard. Hermia may not find her new life as different in that way as she expects."

"I shall find it different enough. It will be free from the forces that crush the impulse of life. That is all that I expect. I can hardly have learned to expect much."

"I wonder how long the feeling will last. It seems a rather indefinite one."

"As long as the conditions here remain. As long as there is the memory of them. And that will be while I live."

"Which is the braver thing?" said Angus. "To do as Hermia has done, or what we are to go on doing?"

"What Hermia has done," said Roberta. "The obvious can be true. What we should not dare to do. We can say that we show the deeper courage. But we know it is the depths of cowardice. Our hearts tell us."

"Courage can take different forms," said Madeline. "We can think of many examples of it."

"Is your own life one of them?" said Hermia.

"We are not always thinking of ourselves and our own lives."

"There is not often much thought left over from them."

"There was one form of courage in this case," said Angus. "And Hermia showed it."

"I am glad I am without it," said Roberta. "To think what I might have to do!"

"To think what Hermia did do!"

"I am not sure that courage is the right word," said Madeline. "Or at any rate the only one."

"I am sure it is," said Hermia.

THREE

"Osbert, you ought to know how to cut a ham."

"Then I do know, Grannie. I only dare to do what I ought."

"Do you expect other people to eat the fat you have left?"

"Is it any good to expect it? Do you think they would?"

"The fat of ham is quite different from other fat."

"That hardly seems worth while when it all has the same end."

"You should cut the fat and lean together, and leave what you can't eat."

"I knew waste was not wicked. That is what I will do."

"What good do you suppose the fat is by itself?"

"No good. Or with anything else. What good could it be?"

"A young man should eat whatever is provided. The fat of ham is quite a wholesome food."

"How do you know? What means is there of knowing?"

"I know from my own experience."

"Grannie, what words are these? Pray do not go any further."

"Can't we forget the ham?" said Osbert's sister. "It dominates the sideboard, but it need hardly do the same to our lives."

"You are late, Amy," said Mrs. Grimstone, turning to the door as a girl of fourteen appeared and came to her seat. "And must you edge into the room as if you were ashamed of entering?"

Her grand-daughter did not explain that she was ashamed of entering at this hour.

"And what a time to come down! Were you not called?"

"Oh I think so, Grannie. Yes, I believe I was. I don't remember."

"I suppose you were so sunk in sloth that you forgot who you were," said Mrs. Grimstone, speaking a true word, if hardly in jest.

"I fear your words may apply to me, Mamma," said a slow, deep voice, as a middle-aged man entered and stooped to salute his mother. "The spirit may have been willing, but the flesh was weak."

"Well, what will you have?" said Mrs. Grimstone, accepting this form of the account, and distinguishing by her tone between a son and a grand-child. "There is hot fish here, and a ham at the side."

Hamilton Grimstone paused and bent his head before making a material choice. He was deliberate over the observance, and raised his eyes as if he had conferred and gained some benefit.

"We have said grace," said his mother, just enunciating the words.

"But I had not, Mamma. And it is not an omission I care to make. One of the penalties of tardiness is the missing of the ritual that inaugurates our day, and without which the day itself is never the same to me."

"What will you have, Amy?" said Mrs. Grimstone, turning from her son, whose beliefs she shared without sharing his pleasure in them.

"Oh, I think some ham please, Grannie."

"I am of similar mind," said Hamilton, with his slow

smile. "But I hesitate to broach the oleaginous mass that obstructs it."

"The fish should be used," said Mrs. Grimstone, in a considering manner, supplying a plate of it for Amy, and meeting a silent acceptance. "It is Osbert who cuts the ham in that way. I have dealt with the matter."

"When matters arise, that is what she does with them," said Erica.

Erica alone of Jocasta Grimstone's grand-children took her on equal terms, and was regarded as qualified to do so. Jocasta did not esteem people for being dependent on herself. She was a tall, upright woman of eighty-four with a small, alert, pallid face, small, penetrating eyes and an air of omniscience which had grown with its long exercise. Her Christian name had been chosen by a parent with more respect for the classics than knowledge of them; and she had accepted it and made it her own.

Her surviving son might have resembled her, had not his lineaments been so overlaid by flesh that the likeness had vanished with them. His pendulous cheeks and chin, pale, globular eyes and almost pendulous frame arrested many a glance. At fifty he might have been any later age, but was seldom guessed to be his own. He had inherited money from a godfather, and gave his time to studying and adding to it, and to consulting his advisers to this end. Jocasta felt to him as her son, but had her own view of him as a man, and was in no danger of her namesake's history.

Her grand-children were of shorter and lighter build, with narrower features and livelier eyes, and a look of covert humour that was fostered by their life. Osbert's features were set a little askew, and gave him an expression in accordance with himself. Erica alone attained to comeliness, and her uncle's eyes recognised this as they rested on her.

31

The three were the orphan children of an unsuccessful son of Jocasta's, and made their home in her house in default of any other. She had educated Osbert and his sister, and articled Osbert to a firm of lawyers nearby, not disposed to afford him more than this, or to esteem him more for his enforced acceptance of it.

"The bell," she said, in an incidental tone.

Her grandson rose and rang it.

"You can take the ham, Hollander," she said to the middle-aged manservant who answered it. "Your breakfast is late this morning."

"We have not eaten or drunk to-day, ma'am," said Hollander, in a tone without expression, as none was needed.

"I said your breakfast was late. You need not repeat it in another form. When a staircase is being repaired you would expect to meet a difference."

"It was by dint of an effort that your breakfast was served as usual, ma'am. The matter was urgent as danger might have supervened."

"I heard it had done so."

"Yes, in the large house, ma'am. A housemaid fell on the broken wood and might have sustained injury if she had not saved herself," said Hollander, his tone recognising her indebtedness to no one else. "As it is the doctor has been called."

"And has come and gone and will come again?"

"Well, ma'am, he is in charge of the case."

"It is not good news. It is most tiresome for Lady Heriot."

"Her vigour may not return in a moment, ma'am," said Hollander, making no change of protagonist. "Owing to its already being used to its limit."

"I might go across and sympathise with Lady Heriot,"

said Jocasta to her family. "We never seem to know them any better."

"There is no question of return to duty, ma'am," said Hollander, more insistently, as if his meaning had not been clear.

"Well, you can take the ham. Some of the fat may have to be cut away."

"Yes, ma'am, to put the edible portion at disposal," said Hollander, standing with his eyes on it.

"I suppose the carpenter has a meal before he goes?"

"It would be assumed, ma'am. If the saying is true, and appearances are deceitful," said Hollander, leaving them with a faint smile on his lips.

"Amy, are you still asleep?" said Jocasta, making no response in kind. "The trap will soon be here. I want to know if Miss Murdoch will be in this afternoon. I may be able to call. I have some questions to ask."

"Oh, she will not, Grannie," said Amy, no longer asleep. "She is very busy just now. There is a good deal to be done."

"She will be free for tea. I will go at that time. Remember to take the message."

"But I never see her, Grannie. She has her tea taken to her room. She is arranging things with the new headmistress and has no time."

"New headmistress? Is Miss Murdoch giving up?"

"No, but she is taking a partner. And they are planning things together. There is to be a good deal of change."

"Oh, I remember the letter now. It seems that a partner is needed. I hope she will serve her purpose. Do you know her name?"

"Oh, it is the name of the people whose housemaid had the accident."

"Heriot? It would hardly be that. It is not a usual name."

33

"It is the one in question, ma'am," said Hollander, now moving round the table. "The eldest Miss Heriot has gone into a school as a partner. The carpenter heard when he went to mend the stair."

"What can be the reason of it? I wonder Sir Robert either allowed it or afforded it. Are you going to do nothing this morning, Osbert?"

"Yes, I am, Grannie. The office is closed to-day."

"Is there nothing in the world but lawyer's work?"

"Not much, as it is coming to seem to me."

"Are you also doing nothing, Erica?"

"Well, what do I generally do?"

"You are too much your father's children. He made no effort and has left no mark. You should take warning by him."

"It seems disrespectful to take warning by a parent."

"Respect has to be earned," said Jocasta, resting her eyes without expression on her other son. "Will you be in for luncheon, Hamilton?"

"Not in person, Mamma. In thought I shall be with you. And with my mind's eye see you at the table with your young group about you. And so enjoy a phantom companionship."

This group, when it gathered, would have been glad for companionship to be of this nature. Jocasta was in the state of nervous strain that occurred in her at intervals without warning or apparent cause.

"No words, if you please!" she said as she came to her seat. "We can eat and drink without them. I have seen it many times."

"So our companionship will be phantom," murmured Erica.

"Let it be," said Jocasta, lifting her hand as if to ward off some hostile force. "Let there be no sign or sound."

34

This condition prevailed and did its work, and later in the day Jocasta left her house and crossed the road to the larger one. Returning, swift and upright, satisfied with herself, she found the world had changed.

"So, Osbert, you have touched the height of humour."

"The words are yours, Grannie. I hardly like to agree."

Whether Osbert agreed or not, someone else did, as Amy's mirth testified.

"Where did you get that skirt? It must have been from my wardrobe."

"Well, yes, that is where it was. Where would a skirt be?"

"That is one of my widow's caps. You must have opened a drawer."

"Well, yes, it is what I do with drawers."

"It ought not to be. There might be something you should not see. People are entitled to their private lives."

"I should have thought they were the last things they were entitled to. I could not think of your having one."

"Is this behaviour typical of your personal life?"

"No, it is an isolated instance."

"I wonder if that is the truth."

"Grannie, do you doubt my word?"

"Well, this surreptitious folly is not so straightforward, is it?"

"Oh, Grannie, have I been dishonourable? The thing I thought I could not be, even in jest."

"Jests can reveal people as much as anything else."

"So they can. Think how mine has revealed me. And how other people's might reveal them. Or rather, keep your thoughts away from it."

"I hope you did not crush the cap?"

"No, no, I treated it with great respect."

"What have you to do this evening, Amy?"

"Oh, I have just to write an essay."

"Just!" said Osbert. "Suppose we all had to write one! Perhaps we can all write this one."

"What is the subject matter?" said Erica.

"Oh, how to spend a day of leisure," said Amy, consulting a notebook.

"How to prevent its being one is what is meant."

Amy did not acknowledge the assistance but gathered her materials and moved away.

"How much have you written?" said Jocasta, after a while. "Come and show me."

Amy sat up and put her hand over the page, her eyes dilating.

"Oh, it is nothing, Grannie. You would see it was. There is nothing there."

"It is enough," said Jocasta. "There can be great silences."

FOUR

"HERE IS A mild surprise for you," said Eliza. "Old Mrs. Grimstone has called. Ostensibly to sympathise about the accident. Really to get a step further with our family. She wants you as friends for her grand-children. And it may do you no harm to know them better."

"Have we to know her better too?" said Angus. "That would do us harm."

"I know what you mean. One does not forget her presence. And there is the usual coincidence. Her grand-child goes to Hermia's school, and she was struck by the name and asked me about it. Hermia's scheme is going beyond itself. It was inherent in it."

"That need do no one harm," said Madeline. "It may even be good for the school. There is no point in keeping it obscure."

"I am not so sure. It can't be too obscure for me. I wish it would fade away. It will always be raising its head. I have just had it thrust in my face. We have done the thing in the best way. But it remains what it is."

"We must be grateful to Mrs. Grimstone," said Angus. "She is helping to keep one of us employed."

"It is not a joke," said Eliza. "You cannot make it one."

"Oh, I thought I had."

"I thought so too," said Sir Robert, smiling. "And we need not be too grave. The piece of strategy won't go far. It is late for change."

"Not too late for Mrs. Grimstone," said Eliza. "She will build on any foundation. She wants the formal relation

37

to become an intimate one. And I don't dislike her in herself. There is nothing against her as a friend. She has her own quality. She is by no means an average woman."

"It seems a many-sided position," said Sir Robert.

"It is. And the sides don't fit. We shall have to steer between them. We will ask the two young people here sometimes. Not too soon and not too often. Just so as to strike the mean and lead to a friendly relation."

"She may not want the mean; and she is used to having what she wants."

"She is certainly a law to herself. In a way I rather respect it."

"So do I," said Angus. "Other people are a law to me."

"Who would have thought Mrs. Grimstone would be a law to Mater?" said Roberta. "I daresay Mrs. Grimstone would. I think it seems she did."

The day came—not too soon, as Eliza had said—when Osbert and his sister were bidden to the Heriots' house. They were shown to the young people and left with them, on the understanding that they were their guests.

"This is our grandmother's idea disguised as yours," said Erica. "And it is a kind disguise."

"It is a most welcome idea," said Madeline. "We have been looking forward to the day."

"We would have done so," said Osbert, "if we were able to look forward. The faculty has faded through lack of use."

"It is not so vigorous in us," said Angus. "We were glad for it to have some exercise."

"Has any of us much to complain of?" said Madeline. "No one should ask too much."

"We don't ask anything," said Erica. "We are guilty for having to receive. We can't be quite without requirements, and that is our proper condition."

38

"We all have to receive. And it is better to be grateful than guilty."

"If we can be one without the other," said Osbert. "We could not."

"Is Madeline pointing out your path?" said Eliza, entering in the cordial spirit she showed with guests. "You will have to get used to our family ways. I daresay you have some of your own."

"We have them instead of anything else," said Erica. "We have nothing but ways."

"What would your grandmother say to that?"

"She would say nothing. She does not answer words that are unwise. It is one of our ways."

"There may be ways in a good many households," said Madeline in a tone without expression.

"Well, it is one of ours to go into luncheon at this hour," said Eliza. "And I hope one of yours to do justice to it. Here is my husband, glad to welcome guests and have a full table. Are you a large family at home?"

"We are five when my little sister is not at school," said Erica. "And when my uncle is with us."

"Oh yes, she is at my daughter's school," said Sir Robert. "It is true that the world is small. Hermia is on fresh ground there. I hope she is walking warily."

"She hardly is," said Osbert. "My sister regards her as a power."

"That is how she would tend to be regarded," said Eliza. "But it is soon to have achieved it. I fear she is going too fast."

"Yes, at lightning speed. The changes are hard on each other. We hear of them day by day."

"I hope your grandmother approves of them?"

"She does not approve of things," said Erica. "It is a thing she does not do."

"Changes have their share of disapproval," said Sir Robert. "It may not be against them."

"It is not in their favour," said Eliza. "And suddenness and self-will are against anything. But I don't know why we talk about the matter. It is not an important one."

"Are we always to talk about important things?" said Madeline. "I suppose everything has its own importance."

"What does your grandmother think of the escapade?" said Sir Robert. "No doubt that is how she regards it."

"It is not as she ought," said Osbert. "She said she respected all useful work when she made me a country attorney."

"No doubt she had her own reasons," said Madeline. "We know she is glad to do all she can for you."

"She does it, and would like it to be more. But I don't think she is glad. She wishes there was no need for it, as we do."

"I am sure you are really grateful to her."

"Are you? She is not. She expresses doubt on the matter."

"Has your uncle a profession?" said Sir Robert.

"No. A godfather left him money and ended the need for one."

"That may not be wholly for his own benefit," said Madeline. "But he is free to share your family life. For you it has its happy side."

"In varying degrees," said Osbert. "Erica has his love, and Amy a modicum of it. I have his recognition that I can't help existing, and his suspicion that I would not help it if I could. In my case he would think the worst."

"Does he manage to fill his time?" said Sir Robert.

"Yes, he does in his own way. He has his great interest and object, his wealth and its increase."

There was a pause.

"I suppose this is a thing I should not say," said Madeline, as she prepared to say it. "But that may result in the ultimate good of you all."

"What good will it result in for him?" said Osbert. "Simply in the present sense of possession. In nothing ultimate at all."

"He may not know that," said Roberta. "It is a thing people don't seem to know. We must hope no one will tell him."

"Suppose someone did?"

"I don't see how anyone could. It would be telling him that one day he would die. And no one tells anyone that."

"He will have to bequeath his wealth," said Angus. "That must suggest its being left behind."

"Has he dared to make a will?" said Erica. "I should not dare to ask him, to seem to picture all he has in other hands. He might never forgive me."

"His life is a contrast to mine," said Eliza. "He can let money do nothing and I have to make it do as much as it can."

"My grandmother would respect you," said Erica. "Indeed she already does."

"I think we respect each other. Our experience and outlook are alike. It seems we have both done and felt more than other people."

"And perhaps they in their own ways have gone further than you," said Madeline, in a light tone.

"Well, we will leave you," said Eliza, rising from the table. "You will like to be by yourselves. We will give you the library until you desert us. And we hope that will not be soon."

When the time came she and Sir Robert entered the hall to speed the guests.

41

"They are a pleasant pair," she said, looking after them. "And on your own mental level. There is nothing against a friendship with them. It should do something for you all."

"We must hope the same will be said on their side," said Madeline, as if this had been forgotten.

"We can't expect to escape judgement," said Sir Robert. "The judge is Mrs. Grimstone, so we certainly shall not escape it. No doubt she is at the moment asking for the account of us."

This was the essential, if not the actual truth. On the return of her grand-children Jocasta looked up and waited in silent question.

"Well, we have been weighed in the balance," said Erica. "And not found too wanting. Lady Heriot found us unexpectedly like themselves. I saw her being baffled by it."

"Why should you be different?"

"I can see some reasons. And so could she. Not of a kind she would mention to us."

"Well, things are on foot at last. It is a step forward."

"That implies steps to follow. And there may be none to follow this."

"We can't tell, and neither can she. These things come about of themselves. They are out of our hands."

"Those that you mean are not out of Lady Heriot's. They are securely in them."

"Well, the future will show."

"We may not be in the future. It is one of the things in her hands. You and she have met your match in each other. And I think she knows it."

"Was any mention made of the daughter's school?"

"There was a little talk of it. Nothing very much."

"She came and listened to the classes to-day," said Amy. "The mistresses didn't seem to like it."

"I daresay not," said Jocasta. "It must have seemed unspoken criticism."

"It was not always unspoken," said Amy with a smile.

"What kind of thing does she say?"

"She wants to change things that have always been done in one way."

"That does not mean it is the best one."

"That is what she says. They say it must be good to have served for so long."

"I think she is right."

"So does she," said Amy, smiling again.

"It is never too late to mend," said another voice, as a slow step was heard. "It appears, Mamma, that that must be her motto. She sounds to me rather a gallant figure. She may be meeting the recognised fate of the reformer. If she fails to reinstate the school, we may be able to account it a great failure."

"I will go to the breaking-up concert," said Jocasta, "and judge of things for myself. And also judge of Miss Heriot. We can't gather much from hearsay."

"I think I might perhaps accompany you, Mamma, and support you in your project. If I should not introduce too discordant an element into the feminine function."

"Oh, there won't be any men there!" said Amy, looking up with startled eyes, her thoughts on her uncle's appearance for which familiarity had had no need to do its accustomed work. "It would really be as you said. Only women seem to come."

"The fathers of the girls are sometimes there," said Jocasta. "I expect there will be a few."

"And in default of a father an uncle may be accepted. As also the spice of variety that he brings. And there will be a protector for Amy and an escort for yourself."

"You would have to sit through the concert, Uncle.

And it will not be at all what you would like. And it is to be a long one."

"I shall hardly attend in a critical spirit, when my niece is doing her best to ease the hours for me."

"Oh, I am not playing, Uncle. No one is to play who is not up to a certain standard. Miss Heriot has been firm about it."

"She is unwise," said Jocasta. "The parents pay fees for flattery, not for firmness, and they have no standard. And it is they whom she has to please."

"She may not recognise the obligation," said Hamilton. "She elects to please herself. Or rather to satisfy her own instinct for quality."

"Oh, it will not be what you think, Uncle. It is just the usual school concert."

"But Miss Heriot is not bound by the usual view of it. Or it seems by anything usual. I have a curiosity to encounter this scorner of convention, both in her family and out of it."

"And now in a girls' school," said Jocasta. "There won't be much scorn of convention there. She will have to come to terms with it."

"An experience that her catholic spirit may lead her to accept. She may even welcome the completion of her knowledge."

"If that is what it is. It is not what was in my mind. I shall be glad to meet her and see how the school is run. I may send Amy to another."

"Would that enhance our position with the Heriot family?"

"No, perhaps not. Well, she can stay," said Jocasta, accepting this view of education. "So you are not to play at the concert? Do you make any progress? Would it be any good to speak to Miss Murdoch or Miss Heriot?"

"No, they can't make me more musical. And I think Miss Heriot might say so. She talks to people as if she was one of themselves."

"She can hardly be called anything else," said Hamilton. "That is the ground I shall take in my intercourse with her."

"Oh, I don't think she would talk to you, Uncle," said Amy, upholding the theory of the meeting as hypothetical. "She will just move about among the people and hardly speak to them."

"I think my conspicuous appearance in the gathering may arrest her attention and lead to an interchange."

"But only for a minute or two," said Amy, who thought the same. "It would just be a word in passing, nothing worth while."

"I flatter myself that I may detain her further. Anyhow, I shall be at your side, Mamma, to meet the redoubtable character."

"What does redoubtable mean?" said his niece, in an empty tone.

"I am not ready with a definition, but I feel it would describe Miss Heriot."

"Then it does what people are not able to."

"Amy, you are not so stupid," said Jocasta. "Why are your reports so poor? Perhaps Miss Heriot will alter them. Though I suppose it would mean altering *you*."

"I am not one of the things she wants to alter."

"Education ought to have some result. Or why does everyone have it? What do you think about it, Hollander? Do you feel it did anything for you?"

"It may have, ma'am, in proportion to what it was."

"You have managed well. You can feel you have had success."

"Well, ma'am, if you would apply the term."

"You have light work and earn a good living," said Jocasta, suggesting that she would.

"It is honest employment, ma'am. And a living as an adjunct can hardly be dispensed with."

"Well, it is not," said Jocasta, as if it was far from being so. "You can have very little to complain of."

"Well, ma'am, it might be a case of nothing or everything."

There was a pause.

"You mean you would choose to do different work?" said Jocasta.

"Well, if there was choice, ma'am, it would hardly fall on the manual. I am not ashamed of a taste for leisure."

"So I have seen," said Jocasta, offering no support to pride in it. "So surely this work is right for you. It is less arduous than most."

"And accorded less esteem, ma'am. I admit I don't concede it myself."

"To what kind of work do you concede it?"

"To that which is done at a desk, ma'am, and nearly approaches leisure. I had no chance of the line myself, and so remain what you see."

Jocasta made no comment on what she saw.

FIVE

"I FIND MYSELF IN a state of trepidation, Mamma. I regret my rashness in imposing my presence on this company. It seems to offer me but a dubious welcome."

"They will be glad to see you. They like to have some men. And I don't want to be alone in this atmosphere. It is more forbidding than I thought."

"Than your memory of it," said a soft, flat voice. "Yes, a memory remains itself. We find it has travelled with us. We are in the power of the past. How do you do, Mrs. Grimshaw? Tell me of yourself."

"Grimstone. No wonder you forget. We have not met for so long. I felt such a stranger here, that I took a moment to recover. It means I should come more often."

Miss Murdoch stood with her eyes on Jocasta's, as if to hold them. She was a small, spare, elderly woman with a deep, grey gaze produced from a plain, lined face, and a suggestion about her that nothing mattered much.

"Ah yes, our paths lie apart. It is when they cross that we see how far apart they lie. And mine is dedicated and yours is free. And that does not draw them closer."

"We should be grateful for the dedication. Nothing else has the same results."

"Results? Are we to think of them? Or to keep our minds from them as points of danger? What do you feel about it? Tell me your thoughts."

"It is best to have good ones in anything we undertake. Or why do we undertake it?"

"And what would good ones be? What do we mean by

47

them? What do you mean? By good ones you mean the most accepted, those that are recognised? That is what you mean?"

"I hope there are some in Amy's case. I would not criticise the kind."

"Amy? Amy Grimstone would it be? Yes, you would share the name. It quivers like a thread through the years and adds to the bond."

"You will let me talk of Amy herself. She has been with you for some time. I hope she gains what she should."

"Gains?" said Miss Murdoch, drawing in her brows. "Gets something for herself to add to her, to be her own? Now, if there is gain, there is giving. We come to what you mean. You mean, do we give her anything? What do we give?"

"Well, perhaps I do. It can be put in that way."

"Time, interest, effort," said Miss Murdoch, looking before her. "They are in our gift. And our hope and thought, our sufferance, if need be. She must gain something I think. Do you not think with me?"

"Well, I hope she must. If so we should see it before long. This is my son, Amy's uncle. You know she has no parents."

"Do I know? Should I have known? Well, it must sometimes be. We take what comes of it. Something must come. We accept it when it is there."

"What would you say it is in Amy's case? It seems that I should know."

"Does it? Or would you look aside? Let others deal with the innocent need, the lack of the natural basis, the want in a young life. It may give its strength. It has been known to give it. I have seen something of difference, a vein of independent thought. Have you seen it?"

"I can't imagine it in Amy's case," said Jocasta, as if

this would prevent it, as it was probable that it would. "She and her brother and sister are the children of the son I lost. I am a widow with a life behind me. I give them what I can."

"What you have left. What you have to give. You give it and can give no more." Miss Murdoch lifted a hand and moved with a muted step towards sounds that heralded the concert. "And it does what it can. It is theirs as it was yours. It is given."

"I fear to take a place from someone with a claim to it," said Hamilton, looking round. "An unbidden guest should remain within his rights."

"They are glad for the seats to be filled. Why should they want them empty?" said Jocasta, taking the one that suited her, and motioning him to her side. "The state of things is clear."

"Then I may feel I am accommodating as well as accommodated," said her son, in an audible tone, looking about him.

"Yes," said Miss Murdoch, with an open smile. "It is clear, and we do not try to disguise it. We let the truth appear. We let it justify itself. We are not afraid of truth."

Jocasta glanced about her, as if she did not under-estimate this courage, and settled down to show the deportment expected. Her son found the quality of the concert as Amy had foretold, and failed to respect its claims.

"Miss Murdoch's talk might be designed to obscure her meaning rather than convey it."

"It might be and is. But leave it for the moment. She notices more than appears."

"Is that Miss Heriot at the side? The tall, dark, up-right woman standing by herself? It seems it must be."

"I think it is. But that is enough. The interval will come."

49

It came, and Jocasta rose and moved to Hermia, with no thought of disguising the purpose of her presence.

"I think you are Miss Murdoch's partner? I am glad to meet you. I hope you can give me a moment?"

"As many moments as you please. They are all my own. Too many to have any meaning. A partner is what I am supposed to be. I hardly know what I am. Miss Murdoch is not afraid of the truth. I will not be either."

"It is not as you thought it would be? Perhaps you put your hopes too high. It took strong reasons on both sides to lead to a scheme like this."

"There was the need of the school for material help. And my father met it. But the reason for me was my own. I was to put the whole thing on another basis, to save its future. I could do it. I see how it could be done. But my help is not wanted or welcome. I am to make no change. And there can't be progress without it."

"It must come to all things in the end. Amy told us you were trying to make it."

"Amy? Your daughter, your grand-daughter? Ought I to know her? Which form is she in?"

"I am not sure," said Jocasta, finding she shared the vagueness concerning Amy that seemed to mark those in charge of her. "The school has a good past. Is there any hope for the future?"

"It depends on the present. And how much hope lies there? Things can't go on as they are. They don't remain at a standstill. Did you notice the standard of the concert? Or pay no attention to it? I hope you closed your ears."

"I will admit I was alive to it," said Hamilton, with a smile. "Ungracious though the admission may sound in someone made welcome to it. I am deriving pleasure from it on other grounds."

"I am deriving it on only one ground. That my family

is not here. It was a struggle to achieve my escape. You would hardly know how great. And a good deal was done for me against the family will. Failure asks more of me than I thought to face."

"And of your honesty and your courage. But I feel neither will fail. We know that both have been tried."

Miss Murdoch approached with hand upraised, indicating return to their seats.

"The high water mark of a concert may be the interval," murmured Hamilton, as they took them. "If it encroached on the time, the gain outweighed the loss."

After the concert tea was handed by the girls to the guests, who were uncertain whether it was a grave or a festive occasion, and were not helped to a decision. Amy chose an unobtrusive part as members of both her worlds were present, and although possessed of two personalities, she had the use of none. Hamilton provided his mother with a seat, and moved about among the guests.

"Who is the man who is with you, Amy?" said a girl.

"Oh, he is some sort of relation who lives with us," said Amy, not prepared to go nearer to the truth.

"Why does he live with you?"

"To get rich more quickly," said Amy, in a confidential manner, dropping her voice. "It saves the expense of a home. Or I believe that is what it is."

"What kind of work does he do?"

"None. He has never done any."

"We heard you call him 'Uncle'."

"Oh, well, we do. He is so much older than we are."

"And he called your grandmother 'Mamma'."

"Oh, he does sometimes. He often does odd things."

"I wonder what the reason is."

"Oh, I suppose it satisfies some kind of want in him," said Amy, lifting her shoulders.

"Perhaps he is illegitimate?"

"No, of course he is not."

"But how can you tell? You would not be told about it."

"Oh, I have heard what he is, but I forget," said Amy, feeling she had better not have done so, and foreseeing problems in the future. "There is no mystery about him, and I daresay he might be worse. I will go and get them some more tea."

"Do you want us to come and help you?"

"No, my grandmother would like me to do it myself," said Amy, fearing filial behaviour in Hamilton, and knowing she must always fear it.

"Here is an arresting sight," he said to his mother, "and I should hazard not a common one. The two headmistresses standing together in conference."

"This is my little grand-daughter," said Jocasta, ushering Amy forward, with a feeling that an introduction might be effected, as one seemed to be needed. "I daresay you will find you really know her."

"No, I shall not. I find I do not," said Miss Murdoch, smiling at Amy. "Knowledge comes with—what shall I say?—with knowledge. When she reaches my form it will come to us, the knowledge of each other. Meanwhile I will not pretend to it. It is not our custom to pretend."

Jocasta did not disagree.

"I know her by sight. I see her when I go through the classes," said Hermia, also smiling at Amy. "I can go so far without pretence."

"And she has seen you," said Hamilton. "And given us an impression of you as far as her powers permit."

"Ah, the powers will grow," said Miss Murdoch. "They will grow as she does, with her, in her, within her range. We are not afraid there will not be growth. It does not fail us."

"It would not do so often. And it does its work without help," said Jocasta, keeping all expression out of her tone.

"Ah, I have said the simple thing. But we do not reject the simple. It is where the truth may lie, and we do not reject the truth."

"At the risk of being simple myself," said Hamilton, as if this was a graver hazard, "I will voice a passing thought. What a pleasure to see the young in holiday garb and mood!"

"Ah, fine feathers do their work. And why should they not? It is what they have to do. The reality is underneath. We get to know the reality."

"And it is a chance to show the feathers," said Jocasta. "Amy was quite moved by seeing her dress brought out. She had thought and felt about it. And she does not usually care about her clothes."

Amy looked aside as if she did not hear, and almost succeeded in not allowing herself to do so.

"Ah, but we should care about everything. It all has its interest, and should all be given it. Indifference is not one of the good things. It must not go through her life."

Amy did not reflect that it need only go through her grandmother's, as the end of the latter receded with every thought of it.

"But the interest will come with time and growth, and the power of choice. This is the stage for simple needs and the simple means to meet them."

"Yes, Amy's needs are of the simplest," said Jocasta, meaning to utter an ordinary word, and actually uttering an innocent one. "She has never had any money of her own. She would not understand what to do with it. She hardly knows there is such a thing."

Amy looked down and rubbed one foot against the

other, using the appearance of a minor discomfort to cover a greater one.

"You might bring your friends to talk to me, Amy. It seems I ought to know them. I never understand why I don't," said Jocasta, unable to feel the matter had been explained to her.

"Oh, they are busy to-day, Grannie. They all have relations here."

"Well, so have you. And they are not tied to them any more than you are."

"Well, some of them seem to be," said Amy, with a shrug and a sigh.

"I might seek an introduction myself in my avuncular character," said Hamilton, unaware that it was his no longer.

"Grannie, Miss Murdoch and Miss Heriot are moving away. Do you want to say any more to them?"

"You must be glad of each other's support," said Jocasta, turning to the partners. "There is a great deal to discuss and decide at a time of change like this."

"What was it that someone said?" said Miss Murdoch. "Someone who had a right to say it. 'There is something a wise man knows. Change is never for the better.'"

"A wiser man would know more," said Hermia. "What of the reforms of the past? We can't say they were anything but what they were. Conscious change is seldom for the worse. There would be no reason for making it. Its object is the bettering of things."

"Ah, what is better? There is the rub, the question that is not answered, the uncertain thing. Is it what seems good to ourselves, perhaps does good? That is what it is?"

"It may be at times. We must judge as we can. It is anyhow better than what seems harmful to ourselves and perhaps does harm."

"I say nothing myself," said Hamilton. "I should not dare to enter the lists with two such able contestants. I will leave my mother in the field."

"Change has to come," said Jocasta. "Though I may be too old to judge of it. This may be the place for it. It is for youth and a school is for the young. Perhaps it should not look too like itself. It may be better disguised."

"It is better still in the open," said Hermia. "If a thing is good it should stand the light. It should seek it and appear as itself, as what it is."

"As you do," said Hamilton, in a low tone. "You appear as yourself, as what you are. An exile from your own world and an alien in this. You have the strength to stand alone. It could not be said of many."

"It can scarcely be said of me. It needs more strength than I know. I am more alone than I thought to be. I tried and failed to live with nothing, and it is again before me. I hardly dare to look forward."

"A house divided against itself," said Hamilton, still speaking to her. "It cannot stand."

"It is true. The slow death will go on. I am losing hope."

"I do not lose it for you. You are young, or young to me. There will be another future."

"There are not so many. For me there was the one. I strove for it and gained it, and it is gone."

Hermia moved away, unwilling to go further with Hamilton, and the voices round them went on.

"Does your grandmother spoil you, Amy? People are supposed to spoil their grand-children."

"Oh, I daresay she does in a sense," said Amy, in a light tone.

"In what way does she spoil you?"

"Oh, everyone does that in a different way," said Amy, aware that Jocasta's method must appear as her own.

"You didn't have a dress for the school play. And it meant you couldn't take part in it."

"Oh, yes, there was a touch of spoiling there. That was an escape indeed."

"And you didn't subscribe very much to Miss Murdoch's Christmas present."

"Oh, I don't suppose Grannie wants to spoil Miss Murdoch," said Amy, with a little laugh. "I think she rather despises her for keeping a school."

"Wouldn't you really rather be more like everyone else?"

"Oh, there are plenty of people to be that. There is no harm in a few exceptions."

"I am glad I am not an exception," said a reflective child, judging the role to be beyond her.

"Why do you not come to see Amy sometimes?" said Jocasta to the girls. "I should like to see her friends about the house. She must not let shyness prevent her asking you. You could sit in the garden and have tea in the schoolroom afterwards. There can be nothing against it."

Amy summoned a smile to her lips at the mention of this prospect, and stood with it hovering over them.

"If I am apprised of the date of the visit I will endeavour to be present," said Hamilton, "and to efface the indefinite impression I have perforce produced to-day."

The girls responded to his smile, and startled his niece who was not prepared for a normal acceptance of him.

"We should like to come and see you, Amy," said one. "It would be a change."

"Would it? I don't know what it would be," said Amy, in an absent tone. "It sounds as if it would be nothing. I shouldn't have anything to do with it. It would be done for me."

"You don't seem to do much for yourself. Do you choose your own clothes?"

"Oh, I don't care about clothes. I never think about them. I wonder people ever do. I hardly know what they are."

The girls held their eyes from the examples before them in case they might hardly suggest this unawareness.

"Your grandmother's clothes are good. She must know what they are."

"Oh, no doubt she does. For Grannie nothing but the best."

"Does she think much more of herself than of anyone else?"

"Oh, well, everyone does."

"I don't think parents always do."

"This is a grand-parent," said Amy, her tone still light, but holding a note of weariness.

"The man whom you call Uncle is your real uncle, isn't he?" said an older girl, using a mild tone to ease the admission. "He is really your grandmother's son?"

"Yes, of course he is. What else would he be? He is her ordinary legitimate son. I said he was not because I was ashamed of him. As I am really ashamed of everything."

Amy had reached the end of her capacity for suffering and was impervious to further cause for it. The girls accepted the feeling of shame as a natural part of life, but glimpsed unusual grounds for it and carried things no further.

"You look tired, Amy," said Jocasta, as they reached home. "It is standing about with nothing in your hands or your head. You get no good out of vacancy."

"No, perhaps not, Grannie," said Amy, accepting the account of her afternoon without surprise.

"How will you feel if the school is given up and you have to go to another?"

"I am not sure, Grannie," said Amy, seeing no prospect of real change unless all schools met this fate.

"Miss Heriot stands by herself," said Hamilton. "And not only in a literal sense. She is indeed an unusual figure."

"Oh, she is not a tragic one," said Jocasta. "She has a home and a family. And would do better to return to them."

"They may be where the trouble lies, Mamma. In a sense they could be the seat of it."

"We will not waste our thought on her. She will not waste hers on us. Nothing is being done for Amy there. And if one of the women has not made an end of the school the two of them will. We will not talk about it. We will not talk about anything. I am worn out and fit for nothing. I must ask for silence."

She leant back and closed her eyes; Hamilton tiptoed from the room; and Osbert began to murmur under his breath.

"She can't have quite what she asks. We must hear what Amy has to tell."

"It is nothing," said Amy, in the same manner. "Or nothing you would understand."

"Was it everything?" said Erica, in a tone that denoted understanding.

"Yes it was," said Amy, in one that accepted it. "I mean it was what Grannie said."

"Could you voice it?" said Osbert. "Even that would be better shared."

"She said I was moved by the sight of this dress. And that I never had any money."

"I hope that was all. It seems to comprise everything."

"No, it was not. She has asked the girls to tea."

58

"Here?" said Erica, on a higher note.

"Here," said Osbert. "It is the unlikely that happens."

"There is nowhere else," said Amy. "It doesn't seem so very unlikely. And the likely really happens oftener."

"It is true. There is no escape. It comes under either head."

"There is something else," said Amy, with a faint smile. "Uncle Hamilton said he would be here. He talked to the girls himself. But he matters less than Grannie."

"Well, he would. She is built on a larger scale."

"Did I or did I not ask for silence?" said Jocasta. "What would this incessant muttering be called? And what are you saying about me?"

"That you are built on a larger scale than Uncle Hamilton," said Erica.

"Well, I may be. I daresay I am. My sons were not equal to me. There is often an outstanding member in a family. But there is no reason why she should be harried to death. You know what I have asked for, and you know I will have it."

As the hush fell, Amy leant back and rested her head on her hand, an attitude that caused her grandmother to frown, though it resembled her own and came from similar feelings.

"Amy, try to look as if you were alive. There is no reason for this exhausted pose. You have had a great deal done for you to-day. Your afternoon has been very different from mine. It seems that pleasure does not agree with you. We must see you don't have too much of it."

"No, yes, Grannie," said Amy, finding she concurred in this view, and hoping that hospitality came under the same head.

SIX

"WELL, HERE I am at home!" said Hermia. "Not where you thought to see me. Not where I hoped to be. Mater is not in the offing? I can say an open word? I am not a welcome figure any more than I am a willing one."

"Why are you at home?" said Madeline, with her eyes and tone grave. "We can hardly be glad of it if you are not."

"Because a break was needed. Because it had to come. Because other things had come. Miss Murdoch and I are like flint and steel. We can't come together without breaking into flame. She holds to her place without the power to fill it. She stands in the way of everything. What I could do is not to be done. What I have done is to be undone. I don't know what the end will be. I begin to feel there must be an end."

"It may be that tact and patience are needed," said Madeline, as if such qualities could not be depended on.

"I told myself that, as everyone would. And I found they did nothing, as everyone does. And I found the decline will go on, as nothing is done to check it. A deadlock has been reached, and is not resolved. I am here for the break to achieve it. Though where my presence failed, it is unlikely that my absence will succeed."

"So you are here again, Hermia," said Eliza's voice. "Sooner than I thought to see you. Not that I felt it would be long. So the school is not the whole of your world? This house is still your background, if not your home?"

"It seems it may be both," said Hermia, in an even

tone. "You sound as if you want me to admit it. Does the admission afford you any pleasure? It affords me none."

"Why, what is the matter? What do you mean? I hope there is nothing wrong."

"I hope so indeed," said Sir Robert, as he came to greet his daughter. "It is soon for a threat of this kind. I trust it is one that will pass."

"The trouble lies deep," said Hermia. "Madeline knows what it is. She will tell you and save me from doing so, and you from hearing it from me."

"I know what it is," said Eliza. "None of us needs to be told. It is what I was afraid of, Hermia. Your temperament has betrayed you. You had great patience here, and it unfitted you for the world outside."

"That is not where I am. I am in a narrower world than this, one where the temperament you mention, or what you mean, was the one that might have served. No other would have been of any good. I could only show it and hope it would prevail. But nothing would or could have. I see there was no hope."

"You showed your temperament and hoped it would prevail. The epitome of your life. And put into words by yourself. We need not say any more."

"How far has the failure gone?" said Sir Robert. "Is it definite and complete?"

"Not either as yet, Father. Or not allowed to be. The threat is not recognised, but it is there. It is best to be open about it. I decided to speak the truth."

"Well, it can seldom be hidden," said Eliza. "In this case it could not be. What has happened to the money we gave? It must have been put to some use."

"Much of it has gone on Miss Murdoch's debts. They were more than I knew. And more than she knew or would know. It was made over to her in payment for my part in the goodwill. I had no control over it. It was not mine."

"No, it was never yours. It was your father's and meant for you all. What a tale for you to tell, and for Angus and Roberta to hear! Are you glad to see them?"

"More than they can be to see me, the tale being as you tell it."

"I was impressed by it," said Angus. "I have a great respect for failure. For letting things pass to other people and having nothing oneself. It is a thing we can speak of openly. It is so much less furtive than success."

"People never speak of that," said Roberta. "And they pretend it is not in their thoughts. There is something shamefaced about it."

"There are other things," said Eliza. "And other things too about failure. I fear that Hermia will find it."

"It is a serious threat," said Sir Robert. "But we took the risk with open eyes. It is of no use to regret it. It is a thing we must sometimes do. But do all you can, Hermia. Try to see Miss Murdoch's point of view. Don't be too sure of your own. The future is largely in your hands."

"It is almost wholly out of them. And it is Miss Murdoch's point of view that is bringing disaster, not mine. It is no good to say any more. You would not be any wiser. There are other matters under the sun. It seems that the post is here."

"With a letter for each of us," said Angus, handing them round. "It is not often so fair."

"Mine is a bill," said Sir Robert. "And it is not at all fair. I have paid it."

"Mine is also a bill," said Roberta. "And it is quite fair. I have omitted to pay it."

"Mine is just from a friend," said Madeline, closing

her lips and her letter after the words in a way that had become accepted.

"Whom is yours from, Hermia?" said Eliza, speaking as one who had a right to ask. "You seem quite lost in it."

"So perhaps she can't emerge from it," said Roberta.

"She must know whom it is from. She can read the signature."

"That seems the end of our duty to a letter," said Angus.

"It is not of her duty to me. Any letters that come to this house are in a sense mine. I have a right to know who is writing, if not what is written. I really have a right to know the whole. Whom is the letter from, Hermia?"

"Just from a friend, as Madeline's is," said Sir Robert, in a light tone. "That is true of most letters."

"Hardly of this," said his daughter, with her eyes still on it. "It is from Hamilton Grimstone."

"Hamilton Grimstone? Mrs. Grimstone's son?" said Eliza. "Why, you don't know him. You can hardly have met. Why does he write to you?"

"He gives his reason."

"Well, what is it? It can't be anything. He is almost a stranger to you."

"He comes with his mother to things at the school. Her grand-child, his niece, is a pupil there. We have talked once or twice, but not in a way to lead to anything."

"To lead to what? Don't make it such a mystery. It can be nothing that matters. Anyhow it is not a secret."

"It might be; perhaps it should be. Some people would make it one, I daresay most people. I shall not. It is a proposal."

"Of marriage? Oh, it can't be. You are making a mistake. You are reading it wrongly. It is out of the question. Let me see the words."

"No, it should perhaps be more of a secret than that. But it is as I said. There can be no doubt."

"Well, if it is, it is a sudden thing. You must have made a conquest. It does happen suddenly sometimes."

Eliza looked at her step-daughter with new eyes. "You did make use of your time, and so did he. Well, it was wise of you both, if you knew your minds. Let me see the letter."

"No, it is surely only for Hermia's eyes," said Sir Robert.

But Hermia put it into Eliza's hands as if she had no personal concern with it, and Eliza read it in a low tone, as though judging of the words. Hermia moved to check her, but desisted and heard with the rest.

'My dear Miss Heriot,
    You will be surprised by my writing to you, and even more surprised by what I write. I should be held to know you very little. But I seem to myself to know you well. And I am venturing to ask you if you will be my wife.
    I can offer material ease, a suitable settlement, and all my feeling.
    If you do not accept my offer I will ask simply and openly that my mother shall not know of it.
        Yours in devotion, if hardly in hope,
                Hamilton Grimstone.'

"Well, so it is the truth. What do you feel about it? I think I like the way he writes. It is a good letter, simple and open and to the point. What do you find your feeling is? I daresay you want time to think."

"No, I know what it is. It is what it would be, a want of it. I am surprised, and I suppose I am grateful, but nothing more. I hardly know him. I don't even like him much. He has shown an interest in me, but I have felt nothing on my side."

"Well, don't decide in haste. Your feelings may respond to his. That is a thing that can happen. This is not a chance that comes every day. You may not have so many. As far as I know you have had very few. You have not been happy of late. You were dissatisfied at home, and the school scheme is hardly a success. It does not leave you with much. And this offers you your own life at a time when you need it, and know your need. You should think and think again. Your tastes may be simple, but you are dependent and used to ease. And we don't know what the future may bring."

"We know enough," said Sir Robert. "There is nothing that necessitates her accepting a man against her will. I have provided for my daughters. Her feelings are the only question. She must judge for herself."

"I have judged, Father, or I have not had to. I could not have a moment's doubt. My surprise at the offer adds to the certainty. I will answer the letter and forget the whole thing as he will wish it forgotten."

"It is a light way to deal with a matter of this moment," said Eliza. "It is a step you can't retrace. You may realise what you are losing, when it is too late. Do not make light of my words. I am not saying them lightly. It is the advice I would give to my own daughter."

"I daresay it is, and it may be sound on the surface. But it has no depth or meaning. Nothing that would count is there."

"How do you feel about it, Madeline?"

"As Hermia does, Mater. There can be no question."

"There can be none," said Sir Robert. "The matter can fall into the past."

"Well, we will leave you to discuss it by yourselves," said Eliza, going to the door. "I don't know what your conclusion will be. We can hear it later."

"She does not know," said Hermia, "though we may think she has been told. She is so used to imposing her view that she can believe in nothing else. And there is the chance of my being disposed of. I see it is becoming a problem."

"Oh, that could only be a secondary thought," said Madeline.

"It may have been, but it was there."

"I look up to you, Hermia," said Roberta. "It is hard to believe in your history. You have escaped from home, a mighty effort, imposed a levy on the family a mightier, met a reverse with quiet courage, won a good man's love and risen to the height of refusing it. Suppose we all lived as fully?"

"And you have not come to the end," said Angus. "You still have to deal with the letter. May I see the answer? Or is it not for any eyes but yours?"

"It had better be only for mine. It can hardly show me to advantage. Refusing something is not a becoming task. It does not put me in the better place."

"I should hardly have thought he had a claim to it."

"Well, perhaps in a sense," said Madeline. "He was anyhow thinking of someone else, and that does not do nothing for it. Though it is hard to see how a deep feeling could arise in so short a time."

"It could for Hermia. We must see it did," said Roberta. "She roused love at first sight, really a rare achievement."

"Especially in a woman of my type," said Hermia, with a smile. "I could see that Mater thought so. She seemed to be viewing me in a new light."

"We must all do that in a way," said Madeline. "It does suggest there is something about you that we missed in our family life. Though that may hardly be the sphere for it."

"For what arouses feeling at first sight?" said Roberta. "No, it is not the sphere. Its opportunities are different."

"We must forget the whole thing," said Hermia. "No one but ourselves is to know about it."

"It is not anything to be ashamed of," said Madeline. "Though perhaps hardly a cause for pride. And I think simple openness is best in everything."

"I am sure it is not," said Roberta. "So many things are better hidden. What of some of our little actions and most of our thoughts? Is simple openness really the treatment for them?"

"Not for the noble ones," said Angus. "We remember when they met it, and the embarrassment it caused."

"I suppose we should not have felt embarrassment," said Madeline.

"Should we ever feel it?" said Roberta. "The instances of it are seldom morally justified."

"Well, is the conclave ended?" said Eliza. "Have you come to your decision? Are you prepared for a change in our family life? We ought to be ready for one. The time is ripe."

"No, no, my dear," said Sir Robert, looking at the faces.

"You know the decision," said Hermia. "And it was only I who had to make it."

"But you made it in haste. You were to reconsider it. Is the result still in the balance?"

"It is what you know. The matter is as if it had not been. It could only have one fate."

"Well, then, there it is, Hermia," said Eliza, in another

67

tone. "You will live your life as you have lived it, in doubt and discontent, always seeking for something beyond your range. And this that falls into your hands, and would give you so much, you cast from you as if it were nothing, as if you had something in its stead. And what have you but a chance that a school may succeed, and a poor chance of that?"

"And a poor thing in itself. I see it as a poor thing. It meant a chance of other things, and may still mean a chance of them. Though, as you say, a poor one. I see it as it is."

Eliza turned and went into the hall and sank into a chair to weep. Her husband followed and she spoke to him through her tears.

"We shall never be free of them, never have our home to ourselves. Always have them here with their judging looks and their set and self-satisfied thoughts. When we were married I did not think of their never leaving us. I thought that in time our home would be our own, that Roberta would be your daughter and would not have the third place. And she will always have it. Things will always be the same."

"It is not her place with me. You know it, and so does she. And I think so do they."

"I am not so sure. They feel they have the prior claim. They say it is their birthright, theirs as a matter of course. Their presence is a part of everything. And I did think one of them might be gone."

"She is doing her best. Your hope is really hers. If she fails it is not her fault. I wish a change could be made, but you know how matters stand. Money is scarce and will remain so."

"Has she made it any more plentiful? My children ask for little and have less. And this chance she thrusts aside, as if it was one of many. And she may never have another. Why should she have had this?"

"Why indeed? There is no reason. She could not care for the man. The offer was a strange one, and acceptance of it would be stranger. We must put it from our thoughts. You know it has not really been in them. And we should go from the hall, my dear. We shall be overheard."

"And the snatches that have reached us are enough," said Hermia. "If we retain any self-respect, we must have had our share. But I daresay we had. It is not an uncommon attribute."

"It is not," said Roberta. "Why are we supposed to have it? It is wasted advice when it is always there."

"Suppose we met someone without it!" said Angus. "It is a good thing to know that we can't. Unless the self-respect goes further and becomes self-esteem, as can sometimes happen."

"I think self-respect is always self-esteem," said Roberta. "I don't know why it is called anything else."

"Should we not try to forget what we have heard?" said Madeline. "We must remember that we overheard it."

"So we should hardly forget it," said Hermia. "But it told us nothing we did not know. Nothing, that is, about Mater. It yielded a little information about ourselves."

"I think it told me something I did not know," said Madeline, in a quiet tone. "That Mater has found us a greater trial in her life than we knew."

"It does not mean that we have found her any less of one. The relation offered little on either side."

"I suppose we should remember she had to bring us up."

"We should hardly forget being brought up by her. I don't need any reminder."

69

"I think she has honestly tried to do her duty by us."

"Under Father's eye. What else could she do? And has she met with any great success? You said we should forget what we heard. You seem to have done so."

"We should be grateful to her for making Father so happy."

"He can be grateful himself for that. It has done less than nothing for us. His infatuation with her has sent an emptiness through our lives."

"I know what you mean. But he has hardly been conscious of it. And ought we to talk like this before Angus and Roberta?"

"Why not? We have always done so. They expect and understand it. And we have not said anything that does not go without saying."

"Then perhaps there was hardly any need to say it."

"Yes, there was need," said Roberta. "There are things that have to be said. Or they might really go without saying. And if that could be borne, someone would sometimes bear it."

"Well, we have had many lessons in our life," said Madeline. "Perhaps more than we should have had in a more usual one."

"And they are seldom happy things," said Hermia. "When someone has had one, it has never been a congenial experience."

"But we may have salutary ones."

"I think you must have, to be so improved," said Roberta. "You could hardly have started like this."

Eliza returned to the room, moved about in silence for a minute, and spoke in a cold tone.

"You seem to have a good deal to discuss. I thought your question was settled."

"You were right," said Hermia. "I am just about to answer the letter."

"Let me see it again and I will dictate the answer."

"No, it would not be mine. And you can't think it should be someone else's, when you see it as you do."

Hermia went to a desk and wrote without delay or pause, and was about to fasten the envelope when Eliza turned.

"The answer must not leave my house without my sanction. I am responsible for what is done under my roof."

"But not for what leaves it."

"Yes, it was written under my eyes and must be worded as I approve. In such a way that the decision is not final."

To the surprise of them all Hermia gave her the letter. They saw it did not reach the foot of the page. Eliza threw her eyes over it.

"Well, so there it is. You have cut away your future. You have chosen subjection and dependence, as if you were fitted for them. And you are not fitted for them, Hermia. You do not know yourself. You have not the qualities needed for such a life. You will live unhappily and uselessly, a trial to yourself and others, until it ends."

"It may be so; perhaps it must be. But it makes no difference. And the matter is only to do with myself. It bears on no one else's future."

"That is true of few things, and not of this," said Eliza, going to the door. "Well, I have said and done all I can. I will weary myself no more."

"Is the letter to go by post?" said Angus, to cover the pause. "Or shall I take it to the house?"

"By post," said Hermia. "It will attract less notice. The episode is at an end. I wish it had not happened. It gives me nothing, and shows my future as it is. It shows it even to me. It is not just what Mater said."

"But there tends to be something in her words that remains," said Madeline. "It is a thing we notice about them."

"It is," said Angus. "She notices it herself. I wonder she dares to speak."

"She does dare," said Hermia. "I am the last to dispute it."

"There is danger in courage. Cowardice is a power for good. We hardly know what it prevents."

"We know what it should have prevented. That is enough."

"If we are thinking of Mater," said Madeline. "Does her courage show a certain quality? She is not ashamed of thoughts and feelings that other people would disguise."

"But why is she not ashamed of them?" said Hermia. "Other people would see the reasons."

"They may get into the way of hiding themselves. And we see she hardly ever does."

"We do. We can't shut our eyes to it. So we are to congratulate her on it. We can hardly congratulate ourselves."

"No, I don't feel you see her quite justly, Hermia."

"Well, how does she show herself to me? And in what light does she see me?"

"Her view of you may partly result from yours of her."

"No, it is the other way round. Her view of me dates from before she saw me. She did not want step-children, and I was the elder and the more to Father. He was to care only for her and her children. And it has almost come to pass. He is not the father to us he should have been."

"He has had his personal fulfilment. We should bear that in mind."

"Our minds are hardly the place for it. We have our own feelings to suffer."

"Yes, it is true," said her father's voice, "and true of us all. My feelings have been what Madeline says. Yours are what we know. And Mater's are what I fear they must be. She advised you for the best as she saw it. Her life has been what it has. And we leave it there. But there is a word for me to say, my dear. Let things be as easy as they may. Old age has come late to me, but it must be at hand. Let me leave peace behind me as the outcome of my days. I once thought to depend on you for more. I thought too far ahead. Life must have its way with us. I see the mistake was mine."

"I think you can depend on me, Father," said Madeline. "I know what you mean and I will do my best. And Hermia will not set herself against me. It is a thing she has never done."

"My trustworthy daughters!" said Sir Robert, putting his arms about them, and remaining as he was with his eyes on the door as Eliza appeared within it. "The future is safe in your hands. I look forward with a quiet mind."

"Why, what is it?" said Eliza with her eyes on them. "What is it all supposed to be? Are you acting some sort of scene?"

"Yes, we are," said her husband, drawing her towards him, and including her in the embrace. "A scene that foreshadows the future, and eases my way towards it."

"Well, we are living in the present now. That will be enough for us. And a scene hardly represents anything when it is on this meagre scale. It leaves out too many of us. It tends to provoke a smile." Eliza proved the tendency and turned aside. "We will go to the library,

Robert. You must learn not to indulge in scenes. I shall be afraid to leave you. You talk of trustworthy people. I wish I could do the same."

She left the room with her husband. The elder daughters also left, and her own two children were alone.

"Suppose the scene had not left us out?" said Roberta. "What would you have done?"

"Comforted myself with awkwardness. I almost did so while I watched it. And it seemed to last so long."

"Yes, every minute seemed an hour. So that is a thing that can really happen. And it must have seemed more to Mater. She could not have managed her emotions in the time. Did you see her face?"

"I did not dare to look at it. My own must have been enough. Father is at an age he should not be. That is the trouble underneath our lives. He has been wise to draw a veil over it. I hope he will not yield to the habit of lifting it. It would not add to his days."

"If only something could add to them! We only know of one method. That of making every minute seem an hour. And that is hardly a good one."

"Well, my dear ones," said Eliza, on the threshold. "So you are sunk in earnest talk. You must try to forget that scene. There was no reason at all to have it. Your sisters should have known better, two mature women as they are. It was absurd for them to be grouped with your father as if they were the foremost figures in his life. As if he saw them in that way! We will put it out of our thoughts. And now this offer of Hermia's and her refusal of it. Can anything be done? Have you any influence with her? I have not sent her answer to the post. The decision is still in abeyance. I cannot have it made certain. It would be a wrong thing to do."

"It would not. It would be a right thing. It is the only

thing," said Angus. "The answer must go to the post as Hermia thinks it has gone. Give it to me and she need not know of its setback. You might be a figure in history, corrupted by power. It is what you are, except that you are not in history."

"It is a pity I am not. It is where I ought to be. I should do a great deal of good. I daresay you will come to realise it. Whose are the voices in the hall? Not your father's and Hermia's and Madeline's?"

But these were what they were, and Angus's voice joined them. And after a minute Eliza's did the same.

"What are you all doing here? What is all the talk about?"

"We are doing nothing. We happened to meet," said Hermia. "The talk is about the letter in Angus's hand. The letter that should be in the post."

"Well, it will soon be there. And it is not where it should be. It should not be anywhere, as you know. I tried to give the matter a chance, and it is taken from my hands. It will be regretted but I can't help it. I have done my best."

"Her best and her worst," said Sir Robert, putting his hand on her shoulder. "It was never in her hands, except in the sense it should not have been. The matter has ended and has never had any meaning. She tried to give it what was not there. Even she could not manage it."

He guided his wife across the hall, and the door of the library closed.

"So there it is," said Hermia. "She can do no wrong. In her own eyes, or in his, or even in Madeline's. The normal rules don't apply to her. She is somehow outside them. It is a wonder she is not worse than she is."

"Well, that is what I think sometimes," said Madeline.

"Though there could be a kinder way of putting it. We might not do as well in her place."

"We know we should do much better. Though perhaps not as well as in a more usual place."

"Or as well as we do in our own," said Angus. "I give myself a great deal of praise in my thought."

"I don't," said Roberta. "I keep my thought away from it. I should take more pride in doing as Hermia has done. We are said to be proud of doing the wrong things, and Madeline may see me as an example of it."

SEVEN

MISS MURDOCH DESCENDED from the Heriots' carriage and stood with her eyes on her partner's home.

"Ah, this is your background. It is what it is and would be. You return to it to breathe a different air. To be restored to yourself and to us."

"Well, perhaps she does," said Eliza, coming with a smile into the hall. "I hope it will do its work. It is true that this house must be called her background. It is the scene of most of her life."

"Ah, is it her reality? Is the time with me the shadow time? Well, it is a part of living and moving onward. It is a forward step, however we see it."

"We hope it is," said Sir Robert, as they went to the luncheon table. "It is to be one in her case, her step towards independence. She is taking it in a serious spirit."

"Ah, I have seen her effort. And I have had my thought and doubt. For effort may be danger, movement that is not forward, something that is just our own."

"This effort is indeed her own. That is why we agreed to it, and did what we could to further it."

"Ah, yes; so she will not put too much on it. Success or failure for ourselves—it is a doubtful thing. Either may take us forward, either take us back. And which of them is the better for us? Is it in our power to say?"

"I feel it is in mine," said Eliza, smiling again. "I would put my faith in success. And I don't feel it would take me back."

"It may not be easy to compare them, Mater," said

Madeline. "There can seem to be so little difference between them."

"I should not have thought often. They tend to be the opposite of each other."

"I suppose extremes may meet?"

"They usually lie far apart."

"Ah, the simple word," said Miss Murdoch. "It serves the simple thing. The simple thought must have its place."

"It must," said Sir Robert. "It is so often in our minds. I think almost always in mine. Indeed it is there at the moment. We are anxious for our daughter to succeed in this venture. I wish I knew there was a chance of it. She is at her best when she has a free hand. May we feel the hope is there?"

"Ah, a free hand, our own way! Do they give it to us, the forces that point our path? And is it a good thing for us, a good thing in itself? Is it a just guide?"

"It tends to be a safe one," said Eliza. "We know our bent and do better when we follow it. But we must not labour our point of view. It is good of you to listen to it."

"Ah, the point of view, the something that is in us, different and deep in us all. Mine comes from the love of the rooted thing, a trust in the past. I will not hide it, will not be ashamed of what I am."

"Are people ever ashamed of that?" said Angus to his sister. "They are always glad to talk about it, whether we can admire it or not. Of course I am not talking of what they are in their hearts."

"They would not count that," said Roberta. "And I don't see why they should. It can make no difference when it is always hidden."

"Ah, you are mockers, innocent ones," said Miss Murdoch, summoning humour to her eyes. "Well, you

78

will be yourselves and go your harmless way. But it is not mine. We shall not go forward together. It would mean acceptance of the surface thought, the surface thing. It may have to come; it may be coming. Let us not think or talk of it."

They did so no more, the occasion wore to its end, and Hermia returned from escorting her guest to the carriage.

"Well, light has broken," she said. "You know the whole."

"There is something I don't know," said Eliza. "Of all the schools in the world, what led you to this one, and to the sacrifice of the family money to it?"

"Its need of the money and of me. The trouble is the failure to make use of them. The picture is complete."

"Miss Murdoch seems in her way an unusual woman," said Madeline.

"She does," said Sir Robert. "It is a safe thing to say."

"She is not unusual in herself," said Eliza. "She has invented a way to seem so. And I daresay it deceives many people, including herself and Madeline."

"It is true," said Hermia. "And people are perceiving the truth. She may have done better at first, when the method was more alive. Before it was an echo of itself."

"Suppose we had met her then," said Angus. "We might have been deceived. I believe I should have been."

"I half thought you were to-day," said his mother. "I was surprised when you opened your mouth. Why do you and Roberta never do yourselves justice with guests?"

"We don't dare to, when the guest is Miss Murdoch," said Roberta. "It is a thing she might not approve. 'Justice to ourselves'; is it a good thing? Worthy of us, worthy in itself? Do we say it is?"

"Hermia and Madeline make the very most of themselves."

"Well, perhaps she does not approve. Hermia does seem somehow to have missed her approval."

"I talked to her a little," said Madeline. "It seemed to be the thing to do. I had no thought of making the most of myself."

"I did the same," said Angus. "And with the same high motive. And I found it was making the very most of myself. And I suppose she saw it. She told me what she thought of me. I could not do the same. But I wished I could tell her that Hermia had had a proposal. We can guess what her response would have been."

"So you need not tell us," said Eliza. "We have had enough of her to-day. And if you and Roberta want to copy someone, why not choose a worthier model?"

"It might mean frustration," said Sir Robert, with a smile. "There would not be a case for mimicry."

"Is there ever a case for it?" said Madeline. "It never gives a fair impression."

"It is true," said Angus. "But we have to be unfair to Miss Murdoch."

"Of course it is easier to be disparaging than to be just. She is very likely quite a good-hearted woman."

"Is disparagement easier than that?" said Roberta. "No wonder we all indulge in it."

"We need do so no more," said Eliza. "We can put her out of our minds. There is one good point about her. She will be easily forgotten. There is nothing definite to remember."

"Hermia may be reminded of her, if they happen to pass at the school," said Angus.

"I shall," said his sister. "But I hope it will go no further. We shall do our best to keep apart."

"And that is how you work together for its good?" said Eliza. "She could see no difference between success and failure. And it seems to be true of you both."

EIGHT

"WELL, I AM alone," said Jocasta. "The saddest thing of all to be. My sons are gone and have no more troubles for themselves. It is I who have them, I who am old and unfit for them. Life can bear hardly on us. Death is the easier thing. Some are marked out for sorrow, and I am one of them."

"For other things too," said Erica. "For freedom and place and power. And the length of days that most of us would choose. Your sons might have put your fate before their own."

"Ah, they would, my sons, the boys who made my youth. They have had too little, torn from me, unwilling to go. Your father was called a failure, but he had much that you had not. It has not been nothing to have you, but it has been nothing compared to having him. I have carried the want of him with me, I shall carry it to the grave. And now the first of them, my Hamilton, the support of my age, cut off by sickness in his prime! Yes, it happens to many, but why to him? Why to him, so content with his own kind of success? It will benefit others and not himself. They will be grateful, but not grateful enough. They will forget who gave them what they have, and take it as their right. I know it; I foresee it. There is nothing I don't know and see. So I will go and be alone. It is what I am. To appear to be anything else is to act a lie. You will be with each other, and I will be with no one. There is no one with whom I can be."

She left them and left a silence, and her grandson broke it.

"We must hope that Grannie will outlive us. Her opinion of people only improves with their death. Few opinions improve much until then, and hers does not improve at all."

"Sometimes she forgets they are dead," said Amy. "And goes back to what she thinks of them."

"It may have been so in Father's case. But it hardly will in Uncle Hamilton's. He leaves her what is his, instead of causing inroads in what is hers. And that will make a difference."

"What will make a difference?" said Jocasta's voice. "I find I cannot be alone. I must be with you who do not want me, and whom I should not have to want. I can't have nothing and no one. I take what is left. That is what my life will be. What will make a difference, Amy?"

"Oh, Uncle's leaving you his money instead of taking yours, Grannie."

"Oh, that is what it is. That is your thought, when he is dead, and my world is dark. Your world is not dark I see, it has a fresh light. When I said I was alone, my word was true. Yes, your uncle leaves what he had. And you will have it in the end. He wanted nothing. It will be for you who want so much, for you who have no right to it. I see it in your faces, the eagerness and the desire. I see it in your eyes."

"No, you don't," said Erica. "It is not there for you to see. It is to you that Uncle leaves what he had. It will belong to you, not to us. We could look in your eyes for the things you imagine in ours. We might say you have told us what they are."

"The money will be mine. But it will not be spent on me. When do I spend money on myself? It will be used

82

for your good or to help your future. And you know it. And the knowledge set your thoughts and feelings working on it. I should like to meet other things in you, but I take you as you are. You have to take me as I am. And I know I am less than I was."

"Can it be true?" murmured Osbert. "Could she ever have been more than this?"

"What was it, Amy? What did you say, Osbert? Something your sister can't repeat. And at this time in our lives! You don't seem to know what time it is. And it would not be fit for me to tell you. I had no thought of the money myself. It is a strange subject for the moment."

"No, it is a natural one," said Erica. "Death must bring money adjustment. It comes, laden with changes, and that is one of them."

Jocasta threw searching eyes over her grand-children's faces.

"There is something I will ask you all. And you will give me true answers. I will begin with you, Osbert. How much do you feel your uncle's death?"

"About as much as he would have felt mine, Grannie. You know what his feeling would have been."

"And you, Erica. How much do you feel it?"

"Perhaps less than he would have felt mine. But that may not be against me. I see it is sad that he is dead."

"And you, Amy. Look at me and tell me the truth."

Amy looked at the ground and told herself the truth, that her uncle would never be seen at school again.

"Oh, I don't know, Grannie; I am not sure. I think I feel as Erica does. It is sad that he is dead."

"It is sad that he is dead," said Jocasta, almost in mimicry. "It is sad that they are both dead, my sons who seemed so apart from each other, and were both so near to me. They had different qualities, perhaps the opposite ones, but their mother understood them and valued them for what they were."

"And knew what they were not," murmured Osbert. "She saw their feet were of clay. And sometimes perceived it in other parts of them."

"What did you say, Osbert? What was it, Amy? Answer me at once when I speak."

"Oh—that you saw their feet were of clay, Grannie; and saw it—perceived it in other parts of them."

"So, Osbert, that is what it was. That is how you talk to your sisters of men who were wiser than you, and are not able to answer. So I saw their feet were of clay? Do you ever turn your eyes on yourself?"

"No, I never do, Grannie. I am made entirely of clay. I ought not to have been made at all. I might see myself as others see me."

"Well, cease to mutter to yourself. Hear yourself as others hear you. If you are ashamed of what you have to say, ask yourself why you say it. Look into your own heart and recognise what you see. There is something different about you all to-day. And it is not a day for betraying the hidden side of yourselves."

"Which days are the ones for that?" said Erica. "I have never known them."

"They say that sorrow is ennobling," said Osbert. "So I suppose Grannie is ennobled. That is why her standard is so high."

"Well, it is my own, and different from yours, perhaps different from everyone's. It is one of the things I have to accept. I must face them and go forward. To fail would be to fail myself. Well, Hollander, you have a sad old woman for a mistress."

"Yes, ma'am," said Hollander, in sympathetic agreement. "When my uncle died my grandmother was never to lift her head again."

"Well, I must try to do a little better than that."

"If you are able to, ma'am. In the other case no hope was entertained," said Hollander with a faint sound of shock in his tone.

"I must think of my grand-children as well as of myself."

"Well, youth has its eyes on the future, ma'am. My grandmother observed it in her dry vein."

"And you don't connect me with the future?"

"No, ma'am," said Hollander, smiling at the idea.

"I may have a little of it."

"Yes, ma'am, with every hour of it an hour too much."

"We should give ourselves to life as long as we have it."

"Yes, ma'am, with thoughts on something very different."

"Perhaps we should not dwell on our own state."

"There would be reminders, ma'am, that would not escape you."

"You think I can turn a clear eye on myself?"

"Yes, ma'am, when that is the direction. Otherwise I think few of us elude it."

"Perhaps I see and feel too much for my time of life."

"Well, ma'am, it is a case of now or never. When you can attend to it, ma'am, a registered packet has come for you. I hope I did right in signing the receipt. The post-man was pressed for time."

"It is from the lawyers. Some sort of document," said Osbert. "What are you engaged in, Grannie?"

"In nothing. It is a copy of your uncle's will. They wrote that they were sending it. There won't be anything to say about it. I know very much what it must be."

"It will only affect yourself," said Erica. "But there may be some minor legacies that will have a human interest."

"It will be short and clear," said Jocasta, as she broke the seal. "There can be no question about it. 'This is the last will and testament of me, Hamilton Grimstone, bachelor, of Egdon House, Egdon, Somerset.' Then some legal formalities and what you call minor legacies to servants and other dependants. And now the gist of the will. 'I give and bequeath to my mother, Jocasta Grimstone, widow, all of which I die possessed in the aforesaid house which she owns and at present occupies. And all else of which I die possessed, namely my investments, securities and moneys at the bank, I give and bequeath absolutely to Hermia Heriot, spinster, of Egdon Hall, Egdon, Somerset, whom I wished to make my wife—' Hermia Heriot! The Heriots' eldest daughter! The mistress of the school! What does it mean? It can't mean what it says. It can't be meant as it stands."

There was a pause. Hollander vanished from the room as if feeling his presence an intrusion, allowing his demeanour to change at the door to one of eager purpose.

"It does mean what it says," said Osbert. "All wills are meant as they stand. And this one stands like this. There is something we have not known. Did Uncle see much of Miss Heriot?"

"He saw her at the school when he went there with Amy and me. He showed an interest in her both before and after they met. Both before and after; that tells its tale; the feeling was half imaginary. It can't have meant anything. He would not have kept it from his mother. What are we to do about it? It is clear that something should be done."

"It seems she must have refused him," said Erica.

86

"Of course she knew him very little. She may not want to take the money. It seems possible that she will not."

"Most people want to take money," said Osbert. "It gives them so much else that they want. This is an unusual case, but it follows the usual line. There is no other for it to follow."

"It is too unusual to be accepted," said his grandmother. "He must have made the will in a mood of emotion, and then omitted to alter it. It is a trouble to change a will. My poor boy, he went through that alone. But it could not have gone deep."

"He may have wished it did," said Erica. "Perhaps he wanted an outlet for feelings he liked to imagine. And he could not know that he was going to die, and that the will would take effect."

"That is another way of saying it means nothing. That is, in itself. Of course it has its legal meaning."

"It has," said Osbert. "And it is the whole of its actual meaning. The money belongs to Hermia Heriot, as his other possessions belong to you. That is how he has apportioned his effects. Is the money very much? Have you any idea of the amount?"

"No definite idea. He inherited a fortune and added to it. He was reticent about the figures, but they were on an unusual scale. If Miss Heriot had known it, and known him better, we can't say what the result would have been."

"But she would not have accepted him," said Amy, unthinkingly, or rather saying what she thought.

"We shall never know what she would have done if she had seen more of him."

Amy was silent on the probable result of this.

"We know nothing," said Erica, "except how he felt to her or wished to feel."

"It is true, poor boy! Oh, Hollander, you are there. You come and go without a sound."

Hollander just smiled and inclined his head, and resumed the occupation he had left.

"How much have you heard of this matter? I suppose you know the whole?"

"It is chiefly snatches that reach me, ma'am," said Hollander, not denying that he was receptive to these.

"We don't want it gossiped about behind the scenes."

Hollander's smile deepened. "No ma'am. If gossip is in question, I am hardly the person to be cited."

"Remember not to mention it. Or have you already done so?"

"No, ma'am, unless an incidental word may have passed my lips," said Hollander, in a tone so incidental that it was hardly articulate.

"It will be all round the neighbourhood. But nothing could prevent it. There are things that can't remain a secret."

"Yes, ma'am. It will not be the word to be applied."

"We need not be conscious about it. There is nothing to be ashamed of."

"No, indeed, ma'am, that feeling is not on your side. The slur of being supplanted should rest on the person who causes it."

"We have no grievance. People can do as they will with their own."

"Yes, ma'am, it seems to be the case. But the word is hardly a misnomer."

"Shall we be much poorer?" said Osbert. "Did Uncle contribute much to the household?"

Hollander continued his movements, but his eyes were still.

"We will talk about all of it presently," said Jocasta, using a weary tone.

Hollander turned as if at dismissal, left the room and closed the door.

"Hollander has had a treat," said Osbert. "A thing that can't be said of anyone else."

"It does seem that Miss Heriot may waive her claim," said Jocasta. "I feel I should in her place."

"Why must we have places of our own?" said Erica. "We should do so well in other people's, so much better than they do themselves."

"There is no reason in her inheriting anything. She can regard nothing as hers."

"People do regard what they inherit as theirs. That is the meaning of inheritance."

"As she did not accept your uncle, she has no moral claim."

"Perhaps she knew she would have it anyhow," said Amy, "and so didn't have to accept him."

"You asked what your uncle gave to the household, Osbert," said Jocasta, disregarding her grand-daughter. "I could hardly enlighten you and Hollander together. He gave nothing but the cost of his support. His interest lay in harbouring what he had; and I understood him and laid no hand on it. He was in his way such a very good son. It means that Miss Heriot inherits more, and we have less than would otherwise be the case. But we shall not be actually poorer. There will be no difference."

"I may come in to finish the table, ma'am?" said Hollander, in a tone between question and statement, acting on the latter assumption.

"Yes, come in. We have no secrets from you. Indeed, I think from anyone. Perhaps there are no such things."

"Well, ma'am, this occurrence would hardly be among them."

"It is a surprise and shock. But it doesn't bear on the real trouble."

"No, ma'am," said Hollander, in sympathy. "Not on the knowledge that after all his feeling was not yours."

"No, I could not think that. I meant the trouble of his death."

"Yes, ma'am, but the heart knoweth. And other words ensue."

"Money is an accidental thing. And we must not grudge Miss Heriot what he wished her to have."

"No, ma'am? I am inclined to do so for you. And in some people the feeling may partake of pity which has an unwelcome flavour."

"Some of it will be sympathy, and we shall be grateful for it."

"Yes, ma'am, if you can place the border line."

"People sometimes like other people to be poorer," said Amy.

"It may be so, miss. I have seen a glint in eyes myself."

"Money played no part in my life with my son," said Jocasta. "Our concern was with other things."

"Yes, ma'am," said Hollander, cordially. "Those being fully at disposal."

"And they were also the deeper ones."

"Money may go with those, ma'am. It is often bequeathed on that basis."

"This is a case by itself."

"And in view of that, ma'am, might the lady relinquish her claim? The idea suggests itself."

Jocasta was silent, knowing it had had no need to.

"What may have been a passing thought, ma'am, can

have results that don't pass with it. You would not see callers to-day, ma'am, I presume?"

"No, not to-day. It is unlikely that anyone will come."

"Well, news travels, ma'am, and questions are on people's lips."

"Hardly on the lips of people who would come here."

"Not in a literal sense, ma'am. But they can be tacit."

"And so can the answers," said Osbert. "I would be responsible for them."

"This news is not known yet. Unless Hollander has already managed to spread it."

"Managed is hardly the expression, ma'am," said Hollander, with a faint laugh.

"We must be prepared for what has to come. And all wills give a wrong impression. Any lawyer would tell you so."

"Lawyers can tell a good deal, ma'am. As one has done to-day. And their news can go to the heart."

"This is hardly bad enough for that."

"Well, ma'am, it has gone to mine," said Hollander, on a sincere note. "It is much for you at this time of your life."

"My time of life may explain it. My son thought he would outlive me."

"And that his secret would remain his own, ma'am. And you would not know that his heart had turned."

"It shows it had not done so. He thought I should escape all this. But what do wills matter? My concern is with himself. I am going away to think of him, and of the others whom I have lost."

"It is a strange thing to happen, Miss Erica," said Hollander, tiptoeing about the room as if Jocasta's presence hovered over it. "And in a way affects us all. A thought more lavishness in the household would not come amiss."

"What would not come amiss?" said Jocasta, glancing back. "What was it, Amy?"

"Oh— a little more lavishness in the household, Grannie."

"In this household? Where people are lapped in comfort from morning to night! So that is what sorrow means for you all, the hope of *lavishness*! That was your thought on losing your master, Hollander."

"No, ma'am, definitely a secondary one," said Hollander, in serious assurance. "It followed merely as a corollary."

"What can you want in this house that you do not have?"

"Well, ma'am, I suppose there are possibilities."

"Well, that would be so in the case of a king."

"That is a position I am not conversant with, ma'am. Gulfs have narrowed, but not to that extent."

There was some mirth, and Hollander's lips twitched, while Jocasta's continued grave.

"You are well housed and fed. And have reasonable time to yourself."

"Is that the life of a king, ma'am? It is scarcely as it is imagined."

"It would describe the life of most kings. Except that the amount of work they do is greater."

"We hear of that, ma'am. There is less said about the amount of work they make."

"The functions that cause it are often the hardest part of their life."

"I should not be surprised, ma'am," said Hollander, half to himself as Jocasta left them.

"Grannie would never spend the money," said Amy,

"any more than Uncle ever spent it. Miss Heriot might as well have it."

"Well, for the moment, miss," said Hollander. "But there is the ultimate future."

"Do you mean when Grannie is dead?"

"I did not employ the word, miss," said Hollander, slightly lowering his voice.

"But you meant when she was dead," said Amy, not modifying hers.

"Well, miss, I put it in my own way," said Hollander.

NINE

"WELL, I COULD have done no more," said Eliza. "What has my life been? Years of care and contrivance, of asking little for myself and accepting less, in order to serve your father and save the family home! And it is all of no good. I might have done nothing, might have lived for myself and forgotten other people, as they have often forgotten me. It is a heart-breaking thing, too much to have to face. And there is support to be given to your father out of my own need. A further demand instead of the help I might have had. I can look to him for nothing. His trouble takes the whole of himself. His heart is in his home and its past. His life is rooted in it. And now its history is broken, and we are to leave it and live at its gates. Strangers will look over us and look down on us for our fall. It takes the meaning out of our lives."

"It can hardly do that, Mater," said Madeline. "Your lives are bound up with each other rather than the place, dear and deeply rooted in them though it is. Your family has come first with you. Think for a moment and you will see it."

"I don't dare to think any further. I have thought and felt enough. My trouble is not for myself. Should I take it as hard as this? The change is too late for your father. It is a drain on strength he is without. And he has to seem equal to it, and carry his usual face. It will all be too much on us both. There seems no hope in anything. I don't know how to go on."

"What is the actual position?" said Angus. "I am in

the dark. Father does the books himself, and I have never really known it. Is there any sudden change? Or any sudden reason for it?"

"The changes have been gathering. They have been gradual rather than sudden. Tithes and rents have fallen; farmers have failed; mortgages have been called in; general costs have risen. The usual troubles of people who live on and off the land. We have never done more than strike a balance, and now the climax has come. We are to leave the family home, that was to be for you and your children's children. There is no entail, and nothing in the way. We are utterly exposed to fate. Well, what is the good of thinking about it? I wish I had not the power of thought."

"I wish you had not. You are being too prodigal with it. We will suffer as little, not as much, as we can. The first will be enough."

"And it is not the worst kind of trouble," said Madeline. "There are many deeper ones. We should try to take it well. We shall still be more fortunate than many people."

"And less fortunate than more," said Eliza. "How many people give up their home and feel a long service to it is wasted? If we took that too well, it would take the life from the past. When trouble comes it is senseless to deny it. There is no courage in shirking the truth."

"I was speaking of facing it, not of shirking it, Mater," said Madeline, in her quiet tones. "There may be a little courage there."

"No doubt there is a difference," said Sir Robert, as he joined them, "though I hardly know which I am doing. I need not say the conventional word, Madeline recognised the occasion for it. 'We still have much to be thankful for'."

"But less than we had," said Roberta, "when we did not think of being thankful. It seems an odd moment to begin it, though I believe it is a common one."

"There will be many moments," said Eliza. "We shall find ourselves the mark of every eye and our misfortune the matter on every tongue."

"There is nothing to be ashamed of," said Madeline. "We must simply be natural and open about it. Do the servants know of the coming change? It seems they should be prepared."

"They must soon be told," said Eliza. "Mrs. Duff is their virtual head. We might send for her and tell her the position, and ask her to explain it to them."

"Do we not owe it to them to explain it ourselves, Mater? It seems a thing they might expect."

"There would be nothing gained. They would not think in that way. And we will do our best for them."

"Is just sending them a word by someone else quite our best, Mater?"

Eliza, as if by way of reply, walked to the bell and rang it. A message was taken to Mrs. Duff asking her to come to the library. She came as if she had expected the summons, and stood with a neutral expression, that threatened to break into expectancy.

"Yes, my lady," she said as Eliza paused.

"There is something we have to tell you, Mrs. Duff, and ask you to explain to the others."

"Yes, my lady, it will not cause surprise. A coming event casts its shadow."

"We would help it if we could, but it is out of our hands."

"Yes, my lady, I will pass it on for you."

"It will take a minute to explain it."

"Yes, my lady, I will pass it on," said Mrs. Duff with a faint sigh.

"You know we have had anxieties of late. Or perhaps you hardly do know. Of course our troubles are our own."

"Yes, my lady, in common with other things. Their nature would vary."

"Well, problems have been gathering. And expenses continue to rise."

"Yes, my lady? In spite of the steps taken to curtail them? In which we have concurred."

"Yes, in spite of those. They have not done much. A real change has to come; we must bow to necessity."

"Yes, my lady, as we all have to at times. Indeed it is at all times for many."

"We are forced to leave this house, the family home for so long, and move to the smaller one near to the main gates."

"Well, it offers an alternative, my lady. It is fortunate that the place comprises a lodge, as need has arisen."

"This house is not a lodge. It has been used as a small dower house, and lately has not been occupied."

"And the accommodation, my lady? Does it suffice?"

"There are two bedroom floors besides the attics. It should be enough."

Mrs. Duff threw her eyes over the group before her rapidly and moved her lips and seemed to be satisfied.

"Well, a move from the large house to the lodge is, so to speak, current, my lady. It is a thing we hear and read of."

"A lodge is a very small house, meant for someone employed. There is nothing we give the name to here."

"There is no need to dignify it, my lady. No family is lowered by moving to the lodge on the place when adversity indicates it."

"It is not the word for this house. It suggests quite a different one."

97

"I find no fault with the word, my lady," said Mrs. Duff, gravely.

"Well, we do," said Sir Robert, less gravely. "We are not making quite such a change. It is enough for us as it is."

"Well, you will explain it to the others," said Eliza, "and tell them how much we regret it, and hope that several of them will still be with us."

"I will do my best for you, my lady," said Mrs. Duff, her tone suddenly without expression.

"Of course they must decide for themselves."

"Yes, my lady, it leads to the best decision."

"We shall not be able to keep all of them."

"Not in the reduced quarters, my lady. It would be the inference."

"And we shall not need them when the work is less."

"Well, my lady, after the stage when it is more."

"That will soon be over. I hope they are not fair-weather friends."

"Well, my lady, there is dependence on both sides."

"They must consider their own welfare. No doubt it is what they are doing."

"Well, my lady, it is how we are all actuated. I will state the case for you. A move to the lodge is necessitated by retrenchment. The change to be accepted or not, as choice dictates."

"It will still be a better place than many. And some people are only fitted for household work."

"Yes, my lady. Or have had no chance of doing any other."

"You will be a support to me, Mrs. Duff? I have not to regard you as an antagonist?"

"It is not the light in which I am seen, my lady. It is help and not hindrance that has been my motto. And I have earned the name."

"It is a noble one," said Angus. "And means you have imagination."

"Well, sir, I am endowed with it. It enables me to grasp the position. And not to be blind to its mortifications," said Mrs. Duff, as she withdrew.

"She ought to be blind to them," said Roberta. "Or anyhow to shut her eyes to them. Her imagination did not go far."

"They are so much on the defensive," said Eliza. "Always up in arms for each other."

"Well, it is natural," said Madeline. "We should not like them so well if they were not."

"I should like them better. I seldom like what is natural; it is usually so unlikeable. People should be civilised. Mrs. Duff has a good home and every consideration. What more can she want?"

"Put yourself in her place, Mater, and answer the question."

"I should not think of it. It would not be fitting. The place is hers, not mine. We don't move people about, even in thought."

"Not other people," said Roberta. "But think of the positions into which we have moved ourselves. Though it is true that Mrs. Duff's is not one of them."

"There is a word to remember through all the easy talk," said Madeline. "The people we depend on have the same feelings as we have ourselves."

"How can we remember it when they have quite different ones?" said Eliza. "You heard the talk with Mrs. Duff. And you will have to suffer some more. She seems to be here again."

"You will excuse me, my lady. Some news has emerged that you may wish to be apprised of. And I felt it would come better from my lips."

"Why, what is it, Mrs. Duff? I hope it is not bad news. Is it something we should know?"

"It can be put in a word, my lady. And I will express it in one. Mr. Hamilton Grimstone has passed on."

"Passed on? Gone away? Left his mother and her family?"

"Well, my lady, he will not again be with them."

"You mean he has died? Tell us what you know. We have heard nothing."

"There is no more for us to know, my lady. Anything further is out of our sphere. Whether or no there is anything, which is a case for divergent opinion."

"But how did it happen? Try to tell us all you can."

"It was a week ago, my lady. Too sudden for the family to be prepared. He was in health, when illness supervened and the result ensued."

"What very sad news! I am troubled indeed to hear it. You are quite right to tell us."

"I felt you would wish it, my lady. And my instinct being a true one I have learned to rely on it. And many people have thanked me."

"As we do, Mrs. Duff," said Madeline. "It must be a sad time in the other house."

"I hear the cloud is a dark one, miss. The news reached me after I left you, and led me to retrace my steps."

"It seems a time of misfortune. But our trouble is nothing compared to this."

"Few troubles are nothing in all eyes, miss. And it may not be the case with this one."

"It is not," said Eliza. "I am glad to meet someone who understands it."

"Understanding has never been my weak point, my lady. It has always thrown light for me, speaking of course of a human standard."

"Oh, surely superhuman in your case," said Angus.

"No, sir. I do not accept it. There is much I am conscious of," said Mrs. Duff, quietly, as she went to the door.

"What a trouble for the Grimstones!" said Madeline. "It does put our own into the shade."

"It does not affect it," said Eliza. "Any more than it is affected by it. Each is as it is. And we had better deal with the problems arising from our own. There are things to be settled in the other house. The rooms are to be assigned, and there is one that is simply a dressing-room adjoining another. One of you will have to manage in it. You must decide among yourselves."

"I will have it, Mater," said Madeline. "So the decision is made. It is a trivial disadvantage enough in the face of our friends' misfortune."

"It will remain when the misfortune has fallen into the past. The dwarfing effect can't continue."

"I am the man," said Angus, "and should take no thought for what I shall put on. I will oust Madeline from her pedestal and occupy it myself."

"We all know who should occupy it," said Eliza. "But I am not going to say it. I can't always do the awkward thing. I will leave it to someone else this time."

"I will do it," said Sir Robert. "It is true that it is time I did. And in this case it is not so very awkward. Hermia will have the room. She is here too seldom for its size to matter. She would say so herself. We can regard it as her decision."

"There is the greater question," said Angus. "What is to happen to this house and all that is in it?"

"The house will be let," said his father. "Not sold, as the future is uncertain. Then after the other house is furnished, the rest of the things must go. We shall be able to keep the best ones."

"And those that are nearest to our hearts," said Madeline. "Some that have no intrinsic value may have another and deeper one."

"They will need space, whatever their value," said Eliza. "And there will not be too much of it."

"Well, space is not everything, Mater. I am sure we shall be equally happy in the other house."

"Why are you sure? I should think there is anyhow doubt of it."

"Happiness does not depend on the size of the rooms."

"It depends on many things. Your father is the one who will suffer. And I shall feel what he does."

"Yes, I fear it is so," said Sir Robert, almost to himself. "This house is a living thing to me. It seems to carry the other lives, whose legacy is in my own. I thought to breathe my last within it. I feel I leave it something of myself. It may be false and foolish and untrue. It is my own truth. I will not hide it as I should betray myself."

"Well, it is something to feel in that way, Father. It is in a sense fulfilment. You can hardly regret it."

"He regrets what it involves," said Eliza. "You heard what he said. And I think so did someone else. There are steps at the door."

"You will excuse me, my lady," said Mrs. Duff. "It seems the case of the bad penny. But there is an item that I felt should be conveyed, as it might be fraught with consequence. Mr. Grimstone has left all he had to a strange young lady."

"A strange young lady? Someone they did not know? Left her all he had! Is it certain? How did you hear?"

"It passed from mouth to mouth, my lady, as it passes from mine now. It was unforeseen and fell on them like a blow."

"To someone who was a stranger to them? What a very unlikely thing! Is there any idea who it is?"

"Rumours are current, my lady. I will say no more."

"Indeed you will," said Angus. "Say some more at once."

"No, sir. Too much has already passed my lips."

"But more has passed other people's," said Sir Robert. "You can tell us what it is. There can be no harm in that."

"It might ensue, Sir Robert. I will not be the one to occasion it. It has never been my tendency."

"You can repeat a rumour, if you say that is what it is."

"Rumour has its name, Sir Robert. I feel my lips should be sealed."

"But they have not been sealed," said Angus. "And you should not deal in half measures. It is an unworthy course."

"The word is yours, sir. My standard is my own."

"It is; that is my complaint."

"You would have known nothing, sir, if I had not been the informant."

"That is true. It is another complaint. I should rather have known nothing."

"I doubt it, sir. It is not the usual preference. Half a loaf is better than no bread. And I am not yet provided with a whole one."

As she withdrew, her hearers met each other's eyes, with uncertain smiles on their lips.

"Well, who dares to say it?" said Sir Robert. "I do not dare."

"Neither do I," said Roberta. "And it was clear that Mrs. Duff did not. It takes more than human courage."

"It may be better not to dare," said Madeline. "When a thing is once out, it can't be unsaid."

"We should not want it to be," said Angus. "What good would it be to anyone?"

"I have the courage to say it," said Eliza. "My courage does not often fail. Life would be different for all of you if it did. I hope you all have the courage to hear it. The name of the young woman in question is Hermia Heriot."

"You can't just say it is Hermia," said Angus. "Your courage does partly fail."

"Do you mean she inherits the money, Mater?" said Madeline.

"I mean it is left to her. What will come of it is another thing."

"Let us all begin to decide," said Angus.

"No, it is better not," said Madeline. "But what a change it may bring!"

"What a change it has brought!" said Sir Robert, looking at the faces round him. "But we must not depend on it. It is only a surmise. There are other young women in the world."

"Not many in Hamilton Grimstone's world," said Eliza. "It is a plausible assumption. It can be accepted."

"It was Hermia he wanted to marry," said Angus. "Not the other young women, or I suppose not."

"Something tells me it is Hermia," said Madeline. "I hear the still, small voice that is seldom wrong."

"Other voices have told you so," said Eliza. "They are often wrong, but in this case there is not much doubt."

"None that matters," said Angus. "It is a good enough foundation. I am ready to build on it."

"We will not do that," said his father. "In any case, the matter is not our concern. No one here has inherited anything."

"It would be in the family," said Eliza. "And we can hardly stand apart from each other. We have shared risk and failure. It would be natural for a debt to be paid."

"Mrs. Duff was right," said Sir Robert, "to say her lips were sealed. She set a good example."

"I don't see why ours should be," said Angus. "Anyhow I am glad they are not."

"So am I," said Roberta. "It would be hard to discern any purpose for them."

"I wonder if Hermia has heard," said Madeline. "She would surely have let us know."

"Heard what?" said Sir Robert, smiling. "What is there to hear or know? There may not be anything. We should assume there is not. But I agree it is a moment of suspense. I wish with you that it was over."

"I think it may be," said Roberta, looking at the door. "I believe it is."

It was. Mrs. Duff entered with a light in her eyes.

"The bad penny again, my lady. But it hardly earns the name. It is good news of which I am the bearer. I have carried it before and felt it, as if it was my own. That is what good news for others is to me."

"But what is this to us?" said Angus. "I fear we are more ordinary."

"The term has not often been applied to me, sir. My dealings bear my stamp. And in this case I can be true and terse. Mr. Grimstone's money passes to our eldest young lady."

"To Hermia," said Eliza, almost to herself.

"To Miss Hermia, my lady, who went out into the world and left her sphere. Her reward has come, and no one would grudge it to her."

"Well, I suppose the Grimstones," said Angus. "It must be the word for their feeling."

"You can use your own words for your own, sir. The occasion warrants it."

"We are glad to know, Mrs. Duff," said Eliza. "It is most unexpected news. How did you hear?"

"The usual channel, my lady. Those that wait upon their house and this. It is a current source."

"I suppose we can depend on it?" said Sir Robert.

"I am told you would do so, Sir Robert, if you had been present in the other house. I put the question and it led to the rejoinder."

"Our thought does go to the family there," said Madeline. "And it meets a sad enough picture."

"Well, miss, if his thought did not go to them, there is no call on anyone else's."

"They may feel they have a moral claim to what he left."

"Well, miss, the other sort of claim is the one that is followed, in my experience. And experience is not a a thing I am without," said Mrs. Duff, as she withdrew.

"What power money has!" said Madeline, with a sigh. "You would hardly expect it to loom so large to Mrs. Duff."

"Why not?" said Angus. "The results of having it or not are before her eyes."

"She is such a useful and respected person. It seems that would be enough."

"Usefulness benefits other people," said Roberta. "And earning respect does much the same. It is when we serve ourselves that we tend to lose it. I hope Hermia will not want too much."

"We know little as yet," said Sir Robert. "Further light may come. It is a strange position. We hardly know if we are glad of it. We will control our thoughts. It is not the time to give rein to them."

"I felt it was," said Roberta. "I have given rein to mine. And I am being carried away by them. We must render to Hermia the things that are Hermia's, and I am rendering them."

"She has a right to what she inherits," said Eliza. "What is the good of a will if it is not to be carried out? It might as well not be made."

"She has a legal right," said Sir Robert. "It could be said that there are others. We must wait to hear her view."

"Which will be her own, and unaffected by yours or mine. We may as well not take one."

"Well, I hardly feel sure of mine."

"What a dubious mood we are in!" said Angus. "One of us inherits great riches and we take it like this. And we were brave over losing our ancestral home. We seem only to be attuned to misfortune."

"We are in doubt about the moral issue," said Madeline. "It deprives the matter of zest."

"Well, the problem is Hermia's," said Eliza. "That is how she will see it. She has always been a person apart. And she is old enough to deal with it herself. Of course she is behind with family events. She does not know we are to leave the house. There has been no time for the news to reach her."

"No, don't connect two different things," said Sir Robert. "They do not bear on each other. Each stands by itself."

"It does," said Angus. "But they have come so near together. And guilty though the thought is, they seem to fit each other. How much does Hermia inherit? Is it known?"

"Not exactly," said his father. "But these things are never quite unknown. A fortune came to Grimstone, and has been accumulating. Hermia is not in an easy place."

"What do you feel she should do?" said Eliza.

"I have said. I find it hard to be sure."

"I don't find anything hard. I am fully capable of certainty. Things should be left to women. They are so much more equal to them than men."

"Well, this matter is left to a woman. And to one who may well be more equal to it than this man."

TEN

"WELL, HERE IS the heroine," said Eliza, "the heiress, or whatever she is. I don't know what to call her. I hardly expected her to look the same. But I can't see any change."

"It is soon for that," said Sir Robert. "But change is on the way. It is the event of a lifetime and must be going deep. We will see it as it is."

"I have hardly done so yet," said Hermia. "It was sudden, and I was unprepared. And I had given up hope of change. But this is not the old sameness with a surface difference. Change is the real word here."

"I hope not too much the word," said Madeline. "The matter should not go too deep. Money is an accidental thing."

"Not in the case of a will," said Roberta. "The rendering up of all we have. There is no element of accident there. I daresay there is almost everything else."

"How did you hear the news?" said Eliza. "We heard it in a roundabout way. I suppose it came formally to you?"

"Yes, from Hamilton Grimstone's lawyer. There was a letter and a copy of the will. I had not heard of his illness. It all seemed so distant from me, for so much to come of it. More and more, as I come to think. It makes a break across my life. I hardly know in which part I live and breathe."

"I can tell you. In the second part. That is to be the one now. The other will sink into the past. This is a matter for the future and must take you forward. You will be another person with another life."

"She will not to me," said Sir Robert. "She has been what she is for too long. She will be the same person with another part to fill. It is true that she will be that. This is a turning-point, and should be seen as such. We will not shut our eyes to it."

"We will not," said Angus. "We will keep them riveted to it. They don't often have such an object."

"I am half-inclined to shut mine," said Madeline. "Money is simply itself to me. I put it and leave it where it should be."

"You do well," said Roberta. "For we find that is where it is. In the pocket and purse of Hermia."

"I wonder what Miss Murdoch thinks about it. I feel she might see it as I do. I suppose she was very surprised?"

"I am sure she sees it as you do," said Eliza. "And of course she was surprised. No one could be anything else. But it will make no difference to her. There will be no change in her life."

"Well, there will in a way," said Hermia. "I am giving up the school. This has somehow led me to it. I don't quite know how or why. I can't give a reason."

"I can," said Eliza. "All this fills your horizon and leaves no room for anything else. It is natural. I should have expected it."

"Now I hardly should," said Madeline. "I feel rather sorry in a way. It seems that your feeling for the school was hardly what we thought."

"It was not what I thought myself, and the thing itself not what I hoped. I needed something, and it was what was there. I will return the money to Father, and the matter can sink into the past. Miss Murdoch can transfer the partnership; and if there is a mild money loss, it hardly matters, as things are."

"So the legacy is large," said Eliza. "The loss would probably not be mild to us."

"It is large. The figures took me aback. I hardly like to state them. I will give them to Father later."

"How I shall like to hear them!" said Angus. "I am so seldom taken aback. Things are always what I expect. I have so much knowledge of life."

"I have even more," said Roberta. "I have tried to avoid it, and that gives us more than anything. It makes us suspicious, and suspicions are always justified."

"I have my share of it," said Madeline. "And of course money is a part of life. I grant it its own place."

"We can trust it to take it. I think it seems to know it. It does not need any help."

"Oh, come, it is not a live thing."

"It is not," said Sir Robert. "But it underlies live things. It is involved with them. We have to accept it."

"What are you going to do with it, Hermia?" said Madeline. "I know the time has been short. But have you any plans?"

"You do give it its place," said Eliza, "and are the first to do so. The future must have time to take its shape. It can't form in a moment."

"It is taking it," said Hermia. "It seems to do it of itself. I hardly have to think of it."

"There is the question of the Grimstones," said Madeline. "What do you think about them? They must feel their position is a strange one."

"As I feel mine is in another way. I know what I think about both. There seems no room for doubt. I recognise their moral claim, as I recognise my legal one. I shall make over half of the money to them, as a former will was in their favour. And the rest is mine to use as I will, for my own or family purposes. That is how I see the matter."

"And as I do," said her father. "I think it is a good way to see it. If I did not agree with your view I should not dispute it. You have a right to it, and the power to form it. But I see the matter with your eyes. It is to me as it is to you."

"She has always been able to judge for herself," said Eliza. "And this calls for the power and brings a use for it. It seems she has been working towards her destiny."

"I am glad the Grimstones are not to suffer," said Madeline. "It would have been the unwelcome drop in the cup for me. It seemed so undeserved."

"It is my part in things that seems to be that," said Hermia. "But I am not going to be troubled. Good fortune has come to me, and I have only welcome for it. I have not always had it. And it will not only serve myself."

"The unwelcome drop in the cup for me is that you are not to have the whole of it," said Angus.

"And for me," said Roberta. "And half of it seems rather a large drop."

"They want you to have all you can," said Eliza, smiling at her children. "It is a good way to feel and would not be everyone's. I suppose it is the right amount for you to give up? Are you sure about it? Have you taken advice?"

"You know she has not," said Sir Robert. "When have you known her take it? This will not alter her, simply give her scope for being what she is. We do not always have it. It is a thing we can't depend on."

"I think I have had it, and been forced to use it. It might have been better for me to have less. It would have saved me from a good deal."

"Have you thought any further, Hermia?" said Madeline. "Or will you live in the moment and leave the future? It seems a natural course."

"It is the right one," said Sir Robert. "The future will move of itself. It holds its own life. There is no need for us to urge it. And there may not be any future. She need not be thinking of any change."

"What I have to do is to prevent one, Father. The one that was coming here. I did not know it was upon us, though I had had my fears. That gives me the line of the future, and there is no need of more than one. I will end the money troubles, and so end the need for the move. That will serve you and me and all of us, and be the thing that is most worth doing, and most asks to be done." There was silence as she paused, and her hearers looked at each other.

"But have you thought?" said Eliza, speaking with her eyes on her husband, as though the words came from them both. "Are you quite sure you have? Thought of yourself and your future? Of your life in the years to come? Regret in the end would be regret on the same scale for us all. You may not want or seek advice, but you need it here."

"The words might be mine," said Sir Robert. "I feel they should have been. See that you hear and heed them. This may be the climax of your youth. You must not lose its meaning for yourself in the onset of family claims, strong and worthy though they be. We can regret our good actions, and it is an unhappy kind of regret. Take care that you do not suffer it. A thing of this kind once done is not easy to undo."

"I should not want to undo it. What is the good of anything that is undone? Few people have any great object in their lives, and I have none. I ask ease and independence, and I could ensure those. And the main thing would be as I have said. Surely too good a thing for there to be any need of a better."

"It is a good thing," said her father. "Too good to accept without doubt. Taking so much from you at such a time must arouse questions in ourselves and of ourselves. I don't know how to answer them. And there is something else to be said. What will be the end for yourself? What might you feel, when other lives were moving on and yours was standing still or running down? The time might come when you saw things as they were. Indeed the time would come. It is possible to be blinded by the zest of giving, when the object is so good. You must think as you have never thought before."

"I have thought, Father. It was clear in my mind from the first. I foresaw the trouble, and could do nothing to help it. It is the better to be able to help it now. As for my own life's doing as you say, it is natural and usual for all lives. I should not think of it."

"Mater and I must think the more. And there is still something else. The position of benefactor might not last. When the money is transferred, the status in a way goes with it. It would be a real giving up. The memory would live, but the ways of memory are what we know. The truth might be in your thought, when it was in no one else's. It would be at times. It is almost a certainty."

There was a pause and Hermia spoke without changing her tone.

"Well, the money need not be legally transferred, if that is too definite a giving up. And if the position of benefactor would be better kept by holding it. I have not anything against the position. I don't suppose anyone would have. And the money could be depended on. There would be no doubt."

"It is for you to say," said Sir Robert. "We should anyhow be taking it from you."

"It is," said Eliza. "And it has been said. By the person who has a right to say it. We know how it is to be."

"We do," said Angus. "And how good it is. We take it from Hermia's hands as from those of a goddess."

"We do. That is how we are to take it. It is not often that something falls from nowhere and confers the place."

"From nowhere? Well, from Hamilton Grimstone. Did he know he was creating a goddess?"

"He recognised one," said Roberta. "And was enabling her to be herself."

"In the event of his death. But he might have lived for years. Why did he not give her some of his wealth in some way?"

"In what way?" said Sir Robert. "By marriage, of course. But the method failed."

"I hardly support the goddess conception," said Madeline. "Hermia is enough for me in herself. Of course I am glad and grateful. It need not be said. But the aloofness is there. I don't disguise it."

"Had you not better try to?" said Roberta. "It seems that would be best. Aloofness from what meets expenses is aloofness from a good deal. It is a great thing that we have a goddess."

"I wish I knew we ought to have one," said Sir Robert. "It is a daughter, a single woman, who holds the place. It is much to be on her, much to take from her, much to owe her in the end. We can hardly know our own thoughts."

"We had better settle them," said Eliza. "They are naturally in confusion. Yours and mine are those that may count the most. Perhaps we could be left to get them clear."

115

Madeline led the way to the door, and the married pair were alone.

"So this is what it is, Robert. This is the change that has come. Hermia is to be over us, to be the giver and the goddess, and have us at her feet. I wish it had not happened. I would rather that things went on as they were, that you changed your home and remained its head. I would rather go to the other house and hold my own and be myself. She did not want to make the sacrifice. I knew she did not want to. She saw the chance to evade it and took it at once. What she is doing is not sacrifice. It is something else. We shall find what it is. We are not to be ourselves, and she is to be more than herself. She is paying for the position. She has been given the means to pay for it. Madeline is right. Money holds too large a place."

"Everything has to be paid for, Eliza. Times and customs change and that does not. I fear it is the truth."

"Only on the surface. We see how little depth it has, when a thing like this comes on us."

"Or how much depth is given it. We know it must be said. And there are other things for me to say. This matter means more to me than it does to you. You fear you will lose as much as you gain; I do not fear it. The house will pass to your descendants and mine; it also comes from my forebears. I should be glad for my son to marry and continue the line; I should not have a mother's loss. In asking you to rejoice with me I am asking much. It is my daughter who is serving us, and not yours; I am asking more. And I ask it, Eliza. Could I offer a greater tribute?"

"You could offer a different one. And one that might serve us all. But you will have what you ask. Hermia will be lifted above us; your daughter and not mine; after all our years together! It is true that you are asking much."

"I am not asking that. We must not think of what we should ask there. It is a loss we share."

"Well, we will leave it there. That is how it is. We go forward together, you on the easier way. I am used to taking the harder one. And now there are things to understand. I am in the dark. Is Hermia to take her old place or to have another? Tell me how it is to be. And do we know the amount of the money, or how she will deal with it, and deal with you? She does not understand how the place is run. She will be as dependent on you as you are on her."

"I don't need to know," said Hermia's voice. "There is not to be any change. The income will pass from my hands to Father's, and the matter will end for me there. I am not altering my place or seeking to modify it. If the legal holding of the money is a safeguard, it may be a wise one. You thought it was, and I knew your thought, and knew what was behind it. We both have our memories of the past. That is all that need be said."

It was a relief that the door opened and another voice was heard; and Hermia left them under its cover.

"You will excuse me, my lady. There is a general message of congratulation. And I am entrusted with it."

"Thank you, Mrs. Duff. I am glad to have it. So your news is up to the moment."

"It has come through, my lady, and been confronted. The old regime to be continued."

"You will say how glad we are that no one is to leave us."

"Yes, my lady. There is no other idea for the present, as far as I know."

"We all share one relief. That we are not banished to the other house."

"Well, my lady, there were compensations. But we are inured to this one."

"I have not heard of those. There has been no mention of them."

"There are points of convenience, my lady. As it were, the hand of the future instead of the past."

"The rooms are very low and small compared with these."

"Yes, my lady, as a lodge would suggest. But the effect was homelike."

"I hope our family uncertainty has not been unsettling."

"Well, my lady, that was the essence of it. And not so unnatural to us. It is the badge of all our tribe."

"In the old days people had to stay in a place for a certain time," said Eliza, accepting the remedy for this.

"Well, my lady, in those days they were hanged for stealing a sheep," said Mrs. Duff, instancing a parallel injustice, as she withdrew.

Eliza was silent for a moment and then left the room with her husband. They met their son and daughter, and she simply made way for them to take her place. Her day was at an end.

"I must ask a question, Roberta," said Angus. "What is your feeling to Hermia? Can you sustain the burden of gratitude?"

"I must. I can only be glad of the cause of it."

"So must I. So we will carry it together. Everything that is shared is halved. And perhaps half our rightful gratitude will not be too much."

"There is something else for us to share. The creeping family uneasiness. Mater will have to show honour to Hermia, and not as to the weaker vessel."

"Well, it can be shared and halved. What a merciful thing it is! I don't think I could have lived through to-day if the feelings had had to be whole ones."

ELEVEN

"'The want of occupation is not rest.
A mind that's vacant is a mind distressed,'"
said Madeline, handing sheets of paper to her guests. "It
is so kind of you to be with us, that we must find something to occupy your minds and save them from distress.
And pencil and paper games will serve the purpose and
not demand too much."

"They can demand enough," said Angus. "Questions
tend to occur in them. And then our minds may indeed
be vacant and distressed."

"I am ashamed to say that I thought a want of occupation *was* rest," said Osbert.

"It is the only kind there is," murmured Amy, smiling
to herself. "Grannie's mind is often occupied. And it is
then that it seems to be distressed."

"There are people whose minds are never vacant,"
said Eliza, giving her a smile. "I belong to them myself;
and I am sure your grandmother does."

"I will belong to them too," said Angus. "Nothing but
the word seems to be needed. And no one would doubt my
word."

"You need not chatter, Amy," said Jocasta. "It is kind
of Lady Heriot to have you here. You can be quiet and
listen to what is said."

"The want of occupation is not to be rest," said
Hermia. "Though it may be better than having to think
of something natural to say."

"I never do that," said Madeline. "I just say what

comes into my mind. It is best to be oneself under all conditions."

"Best?" said Angus. "I think you must mean most honest. And what if nothing comes into your mind?"

"Then I should say nothing. I see no harm in silence. And I think many people would agree."

"I am sure they would," said Eliza, in a neutral tone. "Talking for its own sake has nothing to be said for it."

"Except when it may be seen as a duty, Mater."

"When there is less than nothing to be said," said Roberta. "It is so awkward when people see their duty. There is always the risk that they will do it."

"I should always like to see it done," said Madeline.

"Have you ever seen it?" said Osbert. "I should not dare."

"There are cases in which it is done all the time."

"It is true that there are," said Eliza. "I live in hope of a respite, and never meet one."

"Self-praise is no recommendation, Mater," said Madeline, with a smile.

"I think it is a great one," said Erica. "Who would dare to indulge in it without conspicuous cause?"

"Well, what of my paper games?" said Madeline. "Here is the first of those I had in mind."

"The first?" said Angus. "There are to be more than one? It is true that a mind may be occupied and not distressed. May it be true of us all."

"One of us writes down the first line of a poem, folds over the paper and passes it on. Just as you see me doing now. And the rest of you do the same, until the paper is filled."

"Do we have to make up the line?" said Angus. "I love to show my hidden gifts. It is so sad that they are hidden."

"Would it be cheating just to write the line we are to use?" said Amy.

"You have not to make up anything," said Madeline. "Just write the first line of any poem in print."

"Oh, I can do that," said Angus. "I know some of those. And I should never be drawn to the unprintable."

"And when we have all done it," said Madeline, "one of us reads out the result, and we all laugh at it."

"Do we?" said Roberta.

"A game is what it is," said Eliza. "There is no reason to be serious over it."

"It seems there must be," said Erica. "People are always serious over games."

"No one can win this one," said Amy. "That is why it is different."

"We don't play to win," said Madeline, gently. "We play for the pleasure of the game."

"But it is when people win that they feel pleasure."

"And then they must not show it," said Osbert. "No wonder they are serious."

"What is it we are to do?" said Jocasta, rousing herself from inattention.

"Just write the first line of a poem, Mrs. Grimstone," said Madeline, "and turn down the paper as you see us all doing."

"Madeline spoke with a touch of forbearance," said Erica.

"Well, this is the end," said Madeline, opening the paper. "Now who is to read the lines? I suggest one of the men."

"A task for the stronger sex," said Sir Robert. "I can speak safely as I am disqualified by age."

"I am disqualified by awkwardness," said Osbert. "I could not carry off any general embarrassment."

"I was thinking of Father," said Madeline.

"Well, now you must think of someone else," said Eliza.

"I am disqualified by my respect for letters," said Angus. "In my previous life I was a governess."

"I wonder what I was," said Eliza. "I should guess a general."

"Miss Heriot!" said Amy, with a touch of sharpness, as if the choice was obvious.

"No, I have left the desk," said Hermia. "And in my previous life I was not there."

"So all this comes from writing lines of poems!" said Eliza.

"It seems that anything may come of that," said Roberta.

"What line did you write?" said Eliza with mild interest.

"No, no, Mater," said Angus. "Etiquette must be observed."

"You say you meet no respite from duty, Mater," said Madeline. "So suppose you illustrate your claim and read the lines."

Eliza took the paper, as if almost unconsciously, and rendered the lines with justice both to them and to herself, making what she could of their lack of relation. There was some spontaneous mirth, a renewal of it that was less spontaneous, and a silence that perhaps had the best claim to the word.

"Well, the game was a fair success," said Madeline. "But I hope the next will do better. We all need sheets of paper this time, but I think we all have them."

"May I have another?" said Angus. "I made a rough draft of lines in the middle of mine."

"May I too?" said Amy, glancing at her grandmother. "I began to draw on mine by mistake."

"Your talent must be a natural one," said Angus.

Amy gave him an uncertain glance, and rapidly crushed the paper in her hand.

"I must ask for another," said Osbert. "I tore mine up under the mental strain."

"I gave mine to Father," said Roberta, "because he had made his into a hat and could not get it unmade."

"And now I have lost this one," said Sir Robert, looking bewildered. "And I have not moved from my place."

"It is the paper that has done that, Father," said Madeline. "It is on the floor under your feet. It is too crumpled to use. You must both have fresh ones."

"I have preserved mine in its virgin state," said Hermia. "I don't know if I shall be believed."

"I have done the same," said Erica. "I can hardly believe it myself."

"I have not done anything with mine," said Jocasta, regarding hers as though struck by its blankness. "What ought I to have done?"

"Nothing, Mrs. Grimstone. Just what you have done," said Madeline. "I wish everyone had followed your example. We shall be short of paper. I ought to have provided more."

"We ought to have wasted less," said Erica.

"You should not have wasted any," said Jocasta.

"Grannie has a right to speak," said Osbert. "She took no risks with hers."

"There is paper in my desk," said Hermia. "The desk by the window that I don't often use. I keep it supplied in case of need."

"But that would be good writing paper," said Eliza, looking up. "We keep odd sheets for the games, so that people can use them as they please. There are some upstairs. I can soon get them."

123

"No, no, Mater," said Madeline. "Someone else will do that."

"There is a pile of odd sheets in the desk," said Hermia. "I have never liked wasting paper."

"What have you liked wasting?" said Eliza with a smile. "I somehow don't think very much. The desk is locked and the key has deserted it. I can fetch the paper in a moment."

"I see it as my duty," said Angus.

"Yes, so do I," said his father.

"The desk is not locked," said Hermia. "I have not used it since I lost the key. Anyone can open it."

"But I hope no one does," said Eliza, slightly raising her brows. "Well, of course, I am sure of it."

"Get the paper from the desk, my boy," said Sir Robert.

"No, no, we don't go to desks," said Eliza. "The rule is one to be obeyed. There is reason in it. Angus can run upstairs if I may not."

"I could open the desk myself," said Hermia. "It seems I might have thought of it."

"Get the paper, my boy," said Sir Robert, and said no more.

"Here is a wealth of material," said Angus. "Sheets of all sorts and shapes. I will bring a sheaf of them and hand them round."

"Yes, in a moment, to those who need them," said Madeline. "I will just sort some of them first. Why, Hermia uses the desk more than she knows. There is an opened letter still joined to its empty half. And a recent one to judge by the date. I have not seen any further."

"Well, I suppose not," said Eliza, with a faint laugh. "It is hardly a thing you would do. Why not tear off the written sheet and destroy it? Then there will be no need to trouble."

"No, give it to me," said Hermia. "I don't understand what has happened. I can't use a desk without knowing it. And I have not touched this one for weeks. I suppose there will be an explanation. But I can't think of one."

"Is it a letter that matters?" said Sir Robert, reminded as Hermia sat with her eyes on it of an earlier scene.

"Well, it should have been read and answered, as is the case with most letters. And I have not seen it before. Was there an envelope with it?"

"I think there was. I will get it," said Angus. "I assumed it was a used one that meant nothing. I suppose that is what it is."

"It is what it must be," said Eliza. "There can be no meaning in an envelope. Though I hope the letter still has its point. We will not make a mystery out of nothing."

"It is not what we are doing," said Sir Robert. "The mystery is here. I hope there will be a solution."

"There may have to be a confession," said Eliza, just shaking her head. "And that may not come very readily."

"Here is the envelope," said Angus, "addressed of course to Hermia. There is something in it, this little paper-knife of Mater's. The culprit had no scruple in using what lay at his hand. We all know that knife is sacred."

"He had not much to do with scruple," said Eliza. "The knife is one of the few things that are really my own. It proves he was not one of the family. Not that it needed proof. Well, I daresay no harm is done."

"I hope no great harm," said Sir Robert. "Does anyone know anything?"

"I should say what I know," said Osbert, rising. "I can guess what letter it must be. It is one I wrote to Hermia myself. Anyone can know about it. It is the last thing I could be ashamed of."

"It almost seems we were led to the desk," said Madeline.

"Someone might have been led away from it," said Eliza. "But everything is as it should and would have been."

Osbert met Hermia's eyes and raised his own towards Sir Robert; and she turned and gave the letter to her father. He read it, glanced from her to Osbert and looked away.

"Whatever is it?" said Eliza. "Let us hear and be at peace. We are being teased without any reason."

"It is an offer of marriage," said Sir Robert, "dependent on an answer within a given number of days. It has not been answered, and a refusal is implied which of course means nothing."

"Yes, it is true," said Osbert. "That is how it is. I worded the offer as you say, so that, if Hermia did not accept it, she need send no reply. I had none, and assumed it was not accepted. Now I don't know what to say or think."

"You need do neither," said Eliza. "It is all as if it had not been. You stand as you were before this odd little episode."

"I hope not quite. Hermia had not seen the letter. She has seen it now. I hope there is a difference."

"I am going to offer a solution," said Madeline. "Of course I can only hazard it. Someone opened the letter by mistake, felt guilty and said nothing, but put it where Hermia would find it. He might not even have seen what was in it."

"He probably had not," said Eliza. "A person who opened a letter by accident—and there go we all—might be the last who would read it. His feeling so guilty about it points that way."

126

"Are we sure of the culprit's sex?" said Angus. "Does it have to be mine?"

"I seem to feel it is. I am somehow sure of it. It may be reluctance to attribute the trouble to my own."

"Then it must be someone we employ," said Madeline. "Though one hardly likes to suggest it."

"I think we will not suggest it," said Eliza quietly, "of someone helpless and not here. Now would you all like to return to the games? They may be a protection for those who need it. They would give them cover."

"Is not the moment for them past?" said Jocasta, who had heard in silence, and now turned to say a word to her grandchildren. "Nothing is certain and we will say nothing. Our words might neither add to hers nor become us as guests."

"Grannie has risen on a dead self to higher things," murmured Osbert. "The self we saw earlier to-day was a stepping-stone."

"If Hermia married she would need her income for herself," said Erica. "And might withdraw it from her family. And it applies to other people. Of course there were reasons, and the ruse held no risk. Madeline's solution would have served. But they do not serve me."

"Osbert would surely have tried again," said Madeline.

"He might not," said Hermia, "when a refusal was almost recommended, and for which he had paved the way."

"I was being selfless," said Osbert. "I thought it might strengthen my case."

"Hardly an object to result from selflessness," said Erica.

"I am leaving you for a moment, to give you full freedom of speech," said Eliza. "It seems to me a case for it. You can think or say anything, and even more, say what you think. You can begin with me as the possible culprit, and hold to me if you choose. That would be successful thought and bring credit." She gave a little laugh. "So I leave you to your situation."

There was a pause.

"Only one of us has told us it was she who did it," said Amy gravely. "And we seem to pass it over."

"How did Lady Heriot know what kind of letter it was?"

"How does anyone know that about letters?" said Angus.

"Do you mean she opens them?" said Madeline.

"Tell me of another method," said Angus.

"How did she know it was one that concerned herself?"

"She did not know. She was finding out."

"So you mean she does open letters?"

"No, only those that excite her interest."

"Can you understand her doing it?"

"Yes, I think so. Most letters excite mine."

"But you would not open them?"

"No. I never risk trouble for myself."

"What if you knew no trouble would come of it?"

"I should not like imagining people's thoughts of me."

"But that is trouble. What if there could be none?"

"I like to see myself in a certain way. As free from real guilt."

"Oh, I don't think that need be the word," said Madeline.

"It is the word. What other word is there? It is not as I am. We must all be protected from the truth."

"Is there something you would be afraid of?"

"One thing. Of being found out."

"Yes, of course," said Hermia. "We are all afraid of it. There are things we are right to fear."

"Of course she would have seen it," said Eliza meanwhile to her husband. "Where was it but in her own desk? Why should she have a desk if she did not use it? She can make her own decision now. If she regrets it, it will not be my fault."

"It might have been your fault that she regretted something different. How would you have felt then?"

"That I had tried to save her from something she needed to be saved from. Anything that came of it would only have been what should have come."

"Eliza, we can't take other people's lives into our hands like that. We might do deep and lasting harm. I can only be glad from my heart that we have not done it."

"And what of the other harm that has been done? Will you be glad of that?"

"There can be no harm. None that should be seen as such. People have their lives in their own hands, and we see that they are better there. I wish from my heart that you had not done what you did."

"And what of the other things that I have done? Do you wish I had not done them?"

"You know I am grateful from my heart for them. I have taken them feeling it was safe to take them. Can I feel it is always safe? Was it safe this time?"

"Yes, to my mind it was. I have told you what I can. I will tell you no more. I have said and borne enough."

Eliza broke off at a sound from the door, glanced round and was still for a moment, and then sank into a chair and hid her face in her hands. Sir Robert followed her eyes and met those of Hermia and Osbert, who stood in the doorway with Madeline and the younger pair behind them.

"We came to say we were engaged," said Hermia. "And we have come on something different. Something that is at once to do with it and apart from it. We could not help hearing what it was. We heard before we knew."

"Then I need say nothing," said her father. "There is nothing to be said."

"Father, you are making too much of it. It is hardly what you think. In a way what Mater says is true. When someone is taught through the years that anything she does must be right, it is no wonder if she comes to think that nothing she does can be wrong. In the end harm had to come of it. The real wonder is that it did not come before."

"Then the fault is mine," said Sir Robert, trying to control the change in his tone. "I am to blame and have always been."

"Yes, in a sense you have, and so has she. In another you are both of you innocent though it is an innocence rooted in your wishes for your own lives. We must leave it there."

"I am sure I am innocent," said Eliza, looking up and using her normal tones. "Anything I have ever thought or done has been for the good of you all. And there will be more for me to think and do, if there is to be a wedding on the way."

"And there is," said Sir Robert, moving to embrace his daughter and shake Osbert's hand. "It is the first in our family, and an event in our family life. It will open up the future and take us forward."

"Yes, it will," said Eliza. "A marriage goes beyond itself. It will bring its changes, and they should all be welcome ones. I feel the time is ripe for them."

"It may be, and anyhow the time is good. The first change will be the return of Hermia's money to her own hands. That will be good indeed, both for the reason of it and in itself. It will be welcome to her and to me and to us all."

"No, it would not be, and will not be, Father," said Hermia. "There will be a change, but it will not be that one. I shall transfer the money legally to you, and shall myself have no more part in it. Osbert and I will have enough, and I shall no longer need the protection the formal holding of it gave. I shall be living another life, and shall be glad to do this for the old life and for you before I go."

"I think she is right, Robert," said Eliza, as her husband did not speak. "She has always judged for herself and found the judgement sound. As she says, she will have enough for herself, and she will leave us, feeling that she has saved our future and will continue to save it. In the deeper sense she will hardly be giving more than she gains. It is a great position for her. I should be proud if one of my children had it."

"I am proud that one of my children has it," said Sir Robert, in a quiet tone. "If I cannot be proud of myself I can feel I have a better cause for pride. That is all I have a right to say. My future son-in-law can use his further right."

"It is Hermia's words that stand," said Osbert. "That will be the motto of my life, and I shall need no other. I feel I have used the right."

"It is the motto of all our lives at the moment," said Eliza. "A marriage and the first in the family can only mean what it does. If she will come with me now, we will begin to discuss and arrange it. We can hardly set about it too soon."

She left the room with her step-daughter, and Sir Robert rested his eyes on them, as if appraising their relation. After a minute he followed them, but it was somehow clear that he was going to be alone.

"What do we think of what Mater has done?" said

Roberta to Angus, in a low tone. "Are you ashamed of it?"

"No, of course I am not. I must be worthy of the name of a man. I could not be ashamed of my mother."

"I am not ashamed of it either. Though I don't suppose I have to be worthy of the name of a woman. It is because she is not ashamed of it herself."

"It seems that no one is ashamed of it. Even Hermia is not. Father is the exception, and not a fortunate one. We have seen some real life, Roberta, a thing I have always wanted to see. But now I don't want to see any more. What if I ever experienced any?"

"I don't want to hear any more. What we heard in the moments before they saw us was enough."

"When you say real life, I think you mean life that is deep," said Madeline. "I suppose all life is real."

"Well, I foresee a strange, real thing," said Roberta. "And I hardly think it can be deep. I foresee a friendship between Mater and Hermia. There have always been the seeds of it, and at last they seem to be falling on good ground."

"Well, there could not be a better thing or one more pleasing to Father."

"I am disturbed by it," said Angus. "It is too late for such a difference. I half hope it will not be deep."

"Well, it shows that all things are possible," said Madeline. "And it is sometimes hard to believe that that is true."

"I believe it," said Osbert, "now that I am to marry Hermia."

"What do you think of all that has happened?" said Angus.

"I don't think of it; I should not dare. You surely don't mean that you would dare?"

"Of course he does not," said Roberta. "He belongs

to the family, but you are outside it and might dare."

"No, I belong to it now, and I do not dare. I am proud of belonging to it and not daring. To dare would be the mark of an outsider. I am talking like the family. I quite wish Hermia could hear me."

"Can we imagine ourselves doing what Mater did?" said Angus to Roberta. "We must sometimes face open words."

"I can imagine myself doing almost anything. It doesn't mean that I might do it, or I suppose and hope not."

"Shall we ever be able to trust Mater again?"

"Have we ever trusted her? What would you say? We have given her other feelings, but hardly that."

"Do we feel it matters very much?"

"It matters of course, but other feelings matter too. We may not often have them all."

"Can we ever trust people in a place of power?" said Osbert. "I can hardly say I trust my grandmother."

"And you give her other feelings?" said Angus.

"Well, I give her some," said Osbert, with a smile.

"Will Mater and Hermia trust each other now?"

"Well, Mater will trust Hermia," said Roberta, "because she is worthy of trust."

"I suppose some people must have power."

"Well, some people do have it, and they both use and misuse it. Hermia has had it lately and has used it as we know. I wonder how the two powerful ones are dealing with each other."

These dealings had met with a momentary check as Eliza and Hermia had encountered Cook in the hall, and Eliza had come to a pause as the latter spoke.

"I am glad of the news, my lady. It seems that the spell is broken."

"The spell?" said Eliza, as if she did not understand.

"The spell that condemned the young ladies to single-ness, my lady. It seemed of a relentless nature."

"Oh, that is surely a matter that people must decide for themselves."

"Yes, my lady? If a decision is in question. It might not always be."

"You have not married yourself, Cook," said Eliza, smiling. "The spell has held in your case."

"I have not felt called upon, my lady. Advances have been made."

"People should be able to judge better when they are mature."

"Well, but mature, my lady, in the case of single, young ladies! It is hardly a term to be applied."

"I am in no hurry to lose my daughters. I feel I hardly want to lose Miss Roberta at all."

"No, my lady, that is the face to put on it," said Cook, in approving encouragement as she went her way.

"Cook is disturbed that you and the others have not married," said Eliza, as she rejoined her step-daughter.

"Well, I am disturbed that she has not. We should have had someone in her place, and been spared her talk and its undercurrents."

"I think she is really attached to us all."

"I don't feel it is true affection. She sees us too much as we are. You forget that love is blind. And she forgets it too."

"I wonder how you will manage a house and servants of your own."

"I have always been seen as too managing. There should be no trouble. But I have no wish to learn from experience. I will profit by yours."

They ended their talk and returned to the library, and

134

found that Sir Robert was before them. As he saw them enter together, a light came to his face.

"Here come the two people who in their different ways order my life," he said.

"The ways are very different," said Eliza. "Mine depends on myself, and Hermia's on what fell into her hands from someone else. But happily the hands were the right ones."

"I told you it was coming," said Roberta to Angus, "a friendship between Hermia and Mater. It will put a change through our lives. And no change is wholly good."

"Hermia has bought it dear. She has given up a fortune and forfeited revenge for a wrong done to herself. It is a high price to pay, and Mater can hardly not recognise it. Now there is a question to be asked, that we are afraid to answer. How is Mater facing her return to us after her exposure?"

"It is better not to ask it. If we put ourselves into someone else's place we might as well be in it. And there is everything to be said for keeping out of this one."

"How much courage does she need? We can't help our thoughts."

"More than it is possible to have. She is having to manage without it. And that needs a different courage. And she is not showing any lack of it. And her opinion of herself and what she does may uphold her."

"The same might be said of Hermia. But she does not need to be upheld."

"She does not indeed. She is established on the heights, and Mater is cast down from them. How the first can be last, and the last first!"

EPILOGUE

A Critical Epilogue
by Charles Burkhart

To HEAR, AFTER Dame Ivy's death, that another novel existed, one which rounded out the total to twenty, was the kind of good news to her admirers that the discovery of a forty-second symphony by Mozart might be to almost anyone. To hear, as one did at first, that it was incomplete, was in a different way inviting—because she was the writer one least expected ever to see, in person or *en créatrice, en pantoufles,* in the informality of incomplete creation. But *The Last and the First,* except in a few small ways, is finished, formal, and complete, not at all some vivid glimpse into the laboratory. This is the only way it disappoints. And it seems to show that the conventions of the classical composer are in the grain, they occur from the beginning, they are part of, or may *be,* the originating impulse of the artist. *The Last and the First* is clearly a last work, and not her greatest, because writers of books are not like writers of music, in whom craft and creativity seem to increase through the years in perfect harmony. Many musicians' last works are their best, few novelists' are. But if not her greatest, it is quintessentially her own, and this will be enough for her readers.

The aspects of imperfection consist of those minor omissions and contradictions and repetitions which any writer can find in his manuscript after it has begun to cool. The necessary editing has been confined to a few verbal changes (like "step-daughter" to replace an erroneous "step-mother") and to the construction of one short but essential bridge passage. Other matters she might have changed have been let remain. They have their interest. For examples, both the Heriot and the Grimstone houses have a damaged staircase. Another oddity is that the heads of both families rebuke younger members for their failure to eat the fat as well as the lean of the breakfast sirloin or ham. There are one or two other such parallels. Certain verbal excesses have been let stand, such as the overuse (if it is that) of "with a faint smile" or of "Well"—with which the housekeeper Mrs. Duff begins four out of five consecutive statements. The repetitive "Ah" of the schoolmistress Miss Murdoch is different; she is a lady of maddening manner to which the "Ah" obviously contributes. The changes are minimal, aimed only at intelligibility.

In *The Last and the First* Dame Ivy does what she has always done, and does it well. Here are those familiar conventions that, from the time of *Pastors and Masters* (1925), she has employed to contain and release her vision. *The Last and the First* begins at breakfast: it is when days begin, when conventions begin, and, in her case, when novels begin. We are in a village, which, for once, is named—Egdon, in Somerset; and that we are not in modern times is established, if we had doubted, by references to tithing and to widow's caps. In the opening breakfast scene the usual character of the tyrant is aggressively established, and Chapter I is a monodrama of the tyrant rampant, of Eliza Heriot dominating her 82-year-old husband, Sir Robert, her two step-daughters by his preceding marriage, Hermia and Madeline, and her own children by Sir Robert, Angus and Roberta. "I" is her favourite word ("'. . . I may not be like other people. I begin to see I am not'"). To the pronoun all power and sway of authority adhere: "'I will go into the matter later,'" she says, three times in two pages. There is at least one tyrant in each of the preceding nineteen novels, but in no earlier comment on him is there quite so open and moral a summary as here: "She wielded the power as she thought and meant, wisely and well, but had not escaped its influence. Autocratic by nature, she had become impossibly so, and had come to find criticism a duty, and even an outlet for energy that had no other."

However, the distinctive theme, the significant variation of *The Last and the First* is the overthrow of Eliza by a younger and stronger tyrant, her step-daughter Hermia, and the source of Hermia's strength is money, which she inherits from Hamilton Grimstone, who in his lifetime was her rejected suitor. Money means power: but Hermia uses and will use her power wisely, as Eliza has not. Hermia gives up half her inheritance to the surviving Grimstones, to whom Hamilton in an earlier will had bequeathed his entire fortune, and becomes engaged to be married to his nephew Osbert; with other money she endows Sir Robert and Eliza so that they will not have to leave the house the Heriots have for generations inhabited. The house, as such, is as important here as it is in *A Heritage and its History* and elsewhere. Hermia is a remarkable study of the fledgling tyrant. When we first meet her she has the innate authority, the habit of command, the emphasis and intelligence and irritability. What she lacks is the position itself, and with Hamilton's money, she obtains it. As several members of her family remark, she is now like a goddess; and she is thus like the hero (Hereward Egerton) of the preceding novel, the god of *A God and His Gifts*. At the end of *The Last and the First* (the title refers to Hermia and Eliza), Eliza, whose day, we are explicitly told, "was at an end", who is "'cast down from the heights'", is on cordial terms with the young woman who has defeated her. Money not only breeds power and respect but even friendship. Eliza has always treated Hermia with a more acute attention than the other three young Heriots; she is aware of her larger capacities; and, not ungracefully, she succumbs, after a transparent final manœuvre or two, to Hermia's victory. Her downfall is thoroughly prepared for. Twice she weeps after bouts with Hermia; genuine tears, not stage tears for effect. *The Last and the First* is Dame Ivy's last word on power, on money, on tyranny, and it is her most humane and least intransigent comment.

Most of the novels centre around two households, though not alike in dignity; the secondary household (Grimstone) complements the primary (Heriot), and characteristically attempts to amalgamate with it. It is another of those final resolutions, which seem like softly-heard major chords to inform the atmosphere of *The Last and the First*, that here at last the two households are successfully joined. Though the first attempt by Hamilton to marry Hermia fails, the second, by Osbert, succeeds. The households are alike not only in staircases which need repair; both have tyrants, though Jocasta Grimstone is too wittily observed, by her author and her family, to command Eliza's sway. Her grandson Osbert dresses up in her clothes; of her fatuous son Hamilton we are told that "Jocasta felt to him as her son, but had her own view of him as a man, and was in no danger of her namesake's history". Jocasta has her moments of paranoid splendour—"'There is nothing I don't know and see,'" she says—but, like Sabine Ponsonby in *Daughters and Sons*, she is very old, an aged eagle, and she stoops to attack only intermittently.

Other characters also have, agreeably, their predecessors. No two characters in the novels are ever quite the same; what other novelist has quite Dame Ivy's range and multiplicity of types? The characters which most attract us for their comedy in *The Last and the First* are both like and different from her earlier people. They are Angus, Eliza's son; Hamilton, Jocasta's son; Amy, Jocasta's granddaughter; Hollander, butler at the Grimstones; and Mrs. Duff, housekeeper at the Heriots. Angus is one of those charming and witty people always present in the novels, whose tone is decadent, but who are brilliantly moral, whose apparent decorative uselessness disguises their real function, of speaking truth to the tyrant. They never win. Yet in a sense they never lose because, though the tyrant is barely budged by them, he admits and even encourages their wit. Angus says to his mother, "'You might be a figure in history, corrupted by power. It is what you are, except that you are not in history.'" To which Eliza blandly and honestly replies, "'It is a pity I am not. It is where I ought to be. I should do a great deal of good. I daresay you will come to realise it.'" In a ridiculous poetry game at a party, Angus refuses to read the answers of the players: "'I am disqualified by my respect for letters,' said Angus. 'In my previous life I was a governess.' 'I wonder what I was,' said Eliza. 'I should guess a general.'" The significant contrast is that Angus is a figure, as has been said, of great charm and wit, and a tyrant never possesses either. It is inevitable that Angus should lose the power struggle, but he himself states the consolation: "'I have a great respect for failure. For letting things pass to other people and having nothing oneself. It is a thing we can speak of openly. It is so much less furtive than success.'"

The opposite of Angus's elegant candour is the pomposity of Hamilton Grimstone. Falsity of diction—

pedantry, pretence, the highflown and fulsome—is always a sure guide in these novels to the fraudulent man or woman. When Jocasta asks if he'll be in for luncheon, Hamilton elaborately responds, "'Not in person, Mamma. In thought I shall be with you. And with my mind's eye see you at the table with your young group about you. And so enjoy a phantom companionship.'" When some of his niece Amy's schoolfriends are invited to the Grimstone residence for tea, Hamilton offers to join them: "'If I am apprised of the date of the visit I will endeavour to be present,' said Hamilton, 'and to efface the indefinite impression I have perforce produced today.'"

Her uncle horrifies Amy. Amy is a poignant picture of the suffering adolescent forced into defending herself, her shabby clothes and odd family, against the cold and unsparing insight of her schoolmates. They see her shame and its causes, and its results, her evasions and fibs. Yet Amy is also comic, and occasionally rises to a brusque candid ebullience that shows what she will be like when she reaches maturity. She is not in the least sentimentalised, as a similarly serio-comic figure in Dickens would be.

Nor are Dame Ivy's servants, who more than hold their own against those they serve. The butler Hollander can be compared with the great Bullivant, butler in *Manservant and Maidservant*, and Mrs. Duff with Mrs. Spruce in *Darkness and Day* or with Mrs. Frost in *The Present and the Past*. Not for their similarities, but for the *brio* with which they exist. Both Hollander and Mrs. Duff, though the former is more down to earth and humorous, and the latter more oracular and grand, are dedicated to a pomp of utterance and an elevation of sentiment which are the result of and compensation for their lower positions. Through their agency, news travels between the Heriot and Grimstone households, and their stately decorums of speech are a strange contrast to their chief interest, the recklessly swift transmission of gossip. Hollander is more suave than Mrs. Duff, who is the crustiest of all the cooks and housekeepers. Here she is, in full sail; the subject is the death of Hamilton Grimstone, and Eliza speaks first:

"What very sad news! I am troubled indeed to hear it. You are quite right to tell us."

"I felt you would wish it, my lady. And my instinct being a true one I have learned to rely on it. And many people have thanked me."

"As we do, Mrs. Duff," said Madeline. "It must be a sad time in the other house."

"I hear the cloud is a dark one, miss. The news reached me after I left you, and led me to retrace my steps."

"It seems a time of misfortune. But our trouble is nothing compared to this."

"Few troubles are nothing in all eyes, miss. And it may not be the case with this one."

"It is not," said Eliza. "I am glad to meet someone who understands it."

"Understanding has never been my weak point, my lady. It has always thrown light for me, speaking of course of a human standard."

"Oh, surely superhuman in your case," said Angus.

"No, sir. I do not accept it. There is much I am conscious of," said Mrs. Duff, quietly, as she went to the door.

Not only in characters, but in many another literary

matter, are we on familiar terrain. The plot, never very important in these novels, seems as usual arbitrarily imposed, a mere mechanical framework for the ceaseless talk. In addition to the dominance of dialogue, there are other devices which illustrate once again how much closer her books are to plays than to novels. Here are the usual misplaced document (Eliza, in her farewell turn as tyrant, attempts to hide the letter in which Osbert asks Hermia to marry him) and the overheard conversations: at least a dozen, in which the speakers sometimes casually anticipate being overheard, and are. Another familiarity, the revelation of secrets, is summarised by Jocasta to Hollander: "'We have no secrets from you. Indeed I think from anyone. Perhaps there are no such things.'"

But what these novels are read for is not the violability of documents or the impermanence of secrets. Though her novels are about power and money and death (they are, unfashionably, not about sexuality), it is not even these which primarily attract. She is read for her comedy. Surely these twenty novels constitute the most brilliant and sustained verbal comedy in English. Certainly the most outrageous: "'I suppose this is a thing I should not say,' said Madeline, as she prepared to say it." A new topic is thrown to the actors—the nature of courage, the fireplace in the dining room, the will of Hamilton Grimstone—and they play with it, like acrobats or jugglers, until, and the moment is always immaculately found, its interest is ended. The sentences are now even shorter, plainer, stronger, virtually without imagery or any visual quality. At her very best, her hard human comedy is nearly about nothing; as in the last chapter, where ten different characters have something to say about why they need or do not need another sheet of paper for a game they intend to play. And they say it, though they do not play the game. Words are the best game they play.

The talk is now syntactically so basic that one might not notice how, in this final chapter, she has fully brought together the two families of Heriots and Grimstones for the first time, each of the ten members kept track of and sounding his individual note. As in the case of any deeply classical artist, the surface can deceptively seem thin, yet the more one reads, the more one finds; the more distinctive the characters become, the more powerful their drives and urgent their wit. One begins to realise the symmetries of the narrative, how Chapter VIII begins, "'Well, I am alone,' said Jocasta. 'The saddest thing of all to be'" and Chapter IX begins, "'Well, I could have done no more,' said Eliza. 'What has my life been?'" And that Chapter VIII shows the Grimstones reacting to a misfortune in their family, Chapter IX the Heriots to a misfortune in theirs. It needs no searching, though, to find the wit, still moral and sane and saving, in this twentieth and last novel; like expert swords, in formal exercise, glittering in the empty air.

A Note on the Type

This book was set in Monotype Caslon, a modern adaptation of a type designed by the first William Caslon (1692–1766). The Caslon face has had two centuries of ever increasing popularity in the United States—it is of interest to note that the first copies of the Declaration of Independence and the first paper currency distributed to the citizens of the newborn nation were printed in this type face.

Printed by Halliday Lithographers, Hanover, Mass. Bound by The Haddon Craftsmen, Inc., Scranton, Pa.